W~~ ~~ITH YOU

A STEAMY SMALL-TOWN ROMANTIC COMEDY

SERENA BELL

JMG
JELSBA
MEDIA
GROUP

For Sydney and Soomie.

Copyright © 2022 by Serena Bell

All rights reserved.

Jelsba Media Group

ISBN 978-1-953498-13-7

No part of this book may be reproduced in any form or by any electronic or mechanical means, including information storage and retrieval systems, without written permission from the author, except for the use of brief quotations in a book review.

This book is a work of fiction. Names, places, and incidents either are products of the author's imagination or are used fictitiously. Any resemblance to actual events, locales, or persons, living or dead, is entirely coincidental.

Chipmunk icons made by iconixar from www.flaticon.com

1

JESSA

There should be a special ringtone for calls that suck.

How hard would that be to arrange? After all, most people know when they're calling to deliver bad news, right? They could enter a special code, giving you those few critical extra seconds to brace yourself....

Sadly, the call from my best friend Imani doesn't come with a warning ring tone, just her name and number. I answer it, and Imani says, "I'm so, so, so sorry. I swore I wouldn't be this person."

I'm holding my breath.

"I can't come on the trip."

Nooooooooooo, my inner voice howls.

I am standing in the parking area of Wilder Adventure headquarters, surrounded by a group of people who, like me, are waiting to board the bus that will take us on our wilderness adventure. It's a three-day trip to learn survival skills in relative luxury, compared to the more hard-core trips that Wilder Adventures also leads. I've been super excited since I heard about it, because after my ex-husband Reuben demolished me and left me for roadkill (Kidding. Sort of.), I promised myself I'd get the hell out of my comfort zone this summer. This is my big leap.

Of course, it was going to be a big leap with Imani by my side, but that is apparently not to be. It's just me.

Cue sad emoji and some whiffs of eating alone in the cafeteria in seventh grade.

My big girl self takes a deep, calming breath and exhales for twice as long as the inhale, just in case this turns out to be one of those rare times it actually helps. I need to adult this. Imani wouldn't cancel on me unless she absolutely had to. So if she's calling to bail, she has a totally legit reason. And oh, *shit*, maybe it's something to do with the business?

"Is it The Best Day?"

The Best Day is my wedding planning business. Imani, in addition to being my best friend, is my second-in-command.

"No. It's Jada." She takes a deep breath.

My heart squeezes with worry, my last vestiges of self-pity vanishing. Jada is Imani's adorable daughter and my favorite five-year-old. "Is she okay?"

"She's going to be absolutely fine, but she's in the ER."

"Oh, no! What happened?"

"This morning, she put on my robe and declared that she was Sisu the dragon from *Raya and the Last Dragon*. Which, okay, no biggie, right? But then when I was in the shower, she climbed up on the top of the playhouse, and 'flew.'"

"*Noooooooooooo*," I finally let myself say. At the same time, I'm thinking about Imani's seafoam green fuzzy robe and admiring Jada's costuming acumen.

"They're ninety percent sure it's a broken arm, but we're

waiting to get X-rayed. The thing is, Dan's on a business trip, and I can't get away..." Her voice trails off.

There's only one thing to say. "No, I get it. I totally get it. Of course you can't. She needs her mom with her."

Imani sighs. "I know I'll lose the money, but I have to be here for her."

"Absolutely."

I mean it. Of course I mean it. I'm just—

I'm still feeling clobbered by this year's turn of events, including the world's fastest divorce. And Imani was going to be my buffer against all the things that are scary about this trip. New experiences, personal challenges, and a big social group.

Also, the trip's leader, Clark Wilder.

Who is currently standing to the side of the assembled crew, quietly surveying his territory with intense gray eyes. I swallow my impulse to duck, hide, or whip out a concealed nerf gun and fire it. I try to hold my ground—and his gaze—but fuck, it's hard. The man is a brooding Viking warrior: six-foot-three-ish, with a reddish-brown beard and those I-know-you eyes. In my humble opinion, Clark is the hottest Wilder—and therefore, possibly the hottest man alive.

He also makes me insanely, tongue-swallowingly, nervous.

Shit.

"I'd better go," I tell Imani. "I need to either bail or get with the program."

"Go. Go," she says hastily. "I'm so sorry."

"Please don't stress about it," I say. "These things happen. Give hugs to Jada."

"I will."

I hang up and sneak another look at Clark.

Clark Wilder has rendered me speechless since I first met him. Clark's late wife Emma and I were in a book club together, so I didn't know Clark super well, but I knew he didn't like me. He never met my eyes, smiled, or greeted me with anything other than a grunt.

After Emma died, the book club banded together to support her family and Clark. I brought Clark a pasta bake and tried to hug him, to offer some comfort. He jerked away so abruptly that he dropped the casserole. When we crouched on the floor, scrambling to retrieve it, we bumped heads.

He raised his reddened eyes to me. "Just go."

I got out of there as fast as I could, because there are some moments you can't come back from.

I didn't hold his gruffness against him. I knew it was grief. But a year and a half after that, I ran into him again, at a literacy fundraiser. We were side by side at the food table, him in his dark brown three-piece suit, looking hotter than any man had a right to. "Hi," I said, all ready to give him another chance.

He barely made eye contact. "Hi."

"I'm Jessa Olsen—I was in the book—"

"Yeah. I know."

And then he took his plate and strode away, and a moment later, I saw him chatting with two of his siblings. And laughing.

Ouch.

So, yeah, Clark Wilder doesn't like me a whole lot. Maybe the casserole dropping and head smashing left a sour taste.

I approach him slowly, like you'd sidle up to a dog that

might or might not be friendly (leaning toward not). "Hey," I say.

He grunts. Swear to God. I mean, maybe if you stretch things, it was an "Mmm-hmm," but you'd have to be super generous.

I get a little mad. Well, not mad, exactly, but kind of dug-in. Like, okay, dude, fine, be that way, but you're not going to intimidate me.

I've faced way scarier brides and mothers-of-brides. And admittedly, they're not grunters, but I don't just melt into the woodwork because someone wishes I would.

"My friend's a no-go," I say. "Her daughter's in the ER. Probable broken arm."

He gives me a look that roughly translates to, *Why are you telling me this?*

Really, dude? Seriously?

"I can't get a refund now, can I?"

His eyes sharpen on my face. I have to resist the urge to look away. I stare back at him.

"No refunds."

So now that's three sentences Clark has ever uttered in my presence, maybe four depending on how you count. Well, look at that! He talks!

Then I register what he said.

"Right. Okay."

I weigh my options for a second. Go, and spend two nights on my own without a buddy, in the presence of Mr. Two Words. Or bail, and know I chickened out.

Nope.

Sigh.

"Then I might as well get something out of it, right?"

He shrugs. "Up to you."

Three words! But also, thanks a lot, dude. Way to make me feel welcome.

I do some quick calculations. One, there's the out-of-my-comfort-zone promise I made myself. Two, I'm moving back to the East Coast this fall, and when I do, trips like this will no longer be in my backyard.

"I'm in, I guess."

He nods tightly and turns away from me, and that's the end of our conversation.

"That went well," I murmur to myself.

I survey the group I'm going to be spending the next two days with. Three couples, a group of four women in a tight we've-known-each-other-forever circle, a family of five, three men who arrived together, and the three Wilders: Clark, one of his brothers, and his sister Amanda.

Amanda it is. She's going to be my friend by the end of the weekend, whether she likes it or not.

"Load 'er up!" an authoritative voice commands. Clark. He stands to the side of the mini-bus, supervising the trip goers as we thrust backpacks and other belongings into the undercarriage hold. When it's my turn, I fumble. The backpack straps catch on the edge, halting progress. I struggle unsuccessfully to work my pack free.

My face is turning red with effort and the embarrassment of holding up the line when Clark grabs my backpack like it weighs a quarter of what it does and shoves it into the bay. He's wearing a thin base-layer shirt and a pair of hiking pants that look like they were made for him, and the sight of him bent over and working breaks my brain. I'm still gawping when he turns around. I have to close my mouth and wipe away the drool.

Not really, but it feels like it.

I board the little bus, find myself an empty seat halfway back, and stare out the window, trying to gather my courage. It's not like I'm on one of the primitive survival adventures. This is the Gilderness Adventure—the glamping version of survival. And even though I'm way more at home helping brides find their perfect dress or spec-ing wedding favors, I'm not notably uncoordinated or bad at the outdoors.

Well. I do have a lot of trouble working a compass or reading a map, but the description for this trip assured us we wouldn't be on our own with any of that stuff this time around.

I take a deep breath.

Being uncomfortable is kind of the point, isn't it? If you're outside your comfort zone, it's not supposed to feel easy.

The bus pulls out of the Wilder Adventures parking area, behind a small Wilder-Adventures-branded van. Sadly, Amanda is on the van—a lost opportunity to start my make-friends campaign.

Clark's driving the van, and our bus is driven by Not Clark Wilder. I wish I could be more specific, but whenever someone introduces me to a Wilder brother, I'm too dazzled by his gorgeousness to remember his name. I *think* this one is Kane—one of the younger ones—but I wouldn't put money on it. He has red-and-gold-streaked brown hair and pale blue eyes, and although I'm more of a fan of the Clark Wilder Norse God build, he's a yummy, athletic specimen.

Just as we hit road speed, a walkie talkie crackles a few

seats in front of mine. "Kane?" Clark's voice rumbles over the connection.

So I was right, it was Kane.

"Yeah?" Kane replies.

There's too much static to make out the conversation that follows, but whatever it is, Kane pulls over to the side of the road.

Two people trot up alongside the bus, climb the front steps, and appear in the aisle.

And my heart withers and dies and consumes itself in a crematory blaze.

Okay, I may have exaggerated a tiny, tiny bit.

But it's not good.

Facing me is a woman with lovely honey-colored hair, pulled back in a ponytail. She's packed her perfect, tidy C-cup-ideal bod into a set of expensive-looking hiking pants and a form-fitting base layer. She's the female version of Clark, a fantasy of what an outdoorsy woman should be.

(I wonder if she consulted Pinterest?)

Her name—which I know—is Corinna.

I know her name because she's sleeping with the man standing directly behind her, and has been since well before his divorce.

The man standing directly behind her is my ex-husband, Reuben. He has grown a beard and is wearing a bandana around his head, in a misguided effort to transform himself from artist to hiker. Mostly he just looks like a hack writer with a scraggly beard—which he is.

Sometimes, when confronted with information your brain can't handle, it goes into super slow-mo mode. That's what's happening to me right now. It's like this:

Corinna (who Reuben cheated with) is on the bus.
Reuben (my ex-husband) is also on the bus.
Corinna and Reuben are...
...going...
...on...
...this...
trip.
Together.
With me.
With *just* me.
No Imani.
Noooooooooooo!

Although once again, I make no sound, because the only thing worse than the present situation would be drawing attention to myself.

Corinna and Reuben slide into a seat near the front of the bus.

I could get off. There's probably a rear exit. And surely even a benevolent god testing my resolve about going on this trip wouldn't actually expect me to stick this out.

I test this theory, using the technique taught to me by my divorce counselor: If you were someone else, would you judge her for getting off the bus?

Hell, no.

However. I can see from where I'm sitting that the rear exit of our bus is equipped with an emergency alarm. Which means that if I bail out through that door, the bus will stop, everyone will turn around, and it will be painfully obvious that I've fled.

Corinna and Reuben will see me, and even if they don't, Clark will tell them. ("Oh, yeah, that was Jessa Olsen who went out the back. I have no idea where she's going, but who needs her, anyway?")

Then it would be obvious to Reuben that I didn't have the courage to stick this out. And given what he's already taken from me, he doesn't deserve that satisfaction.

I slink down in my seat and hide, wishing I could disappear, but the best superpower I've got at this moment is access to the snack bar in my jacket pocket.

2

CLARK

"Is this seat taken?"

The questioner is my sister Amanda, and the seat being referenced is the one directly behind the driver's seat of the van, where I'm sitting. She knows the answer; she's just asking it to bust my ass. Busting Wilder brothers' asses is one of Amanda's reasons for living.

"Yes, it is," I lie. "Go sit on the bus."

She sits there anyway, of course. She and I are the only two in the van; everyone else is on the bus. But the van's seats are crammed with gear, and we need two vehicles at the trailhead in case there's an emergency.

"Go harass someone else," I tell her.

"Who says I'm going to harass you?"

"Past experience."

"You're supposed to be falling all over yourself with gratitude because Kane and I volunteered to help you with this trip," she points out, reasonably.

It's true. Gabe and Lucy are my usual partners for these Gilderness outings, and I am, on paper, lucky that Amanda and

Kane volunteered to take over when Gabe and Lucy had somewhere else to be. Amanda was able to take a few days off from her catering business and leave her three kiddos in care of her husband Heath, and Kane's ski-and-snowshoe-tour business is quiet enough in the summer that his partner, Hanna, could easily handle things without him. Thank God, because leading one of these Gilderness beasts is way too big a job for one guy.

I'd like to say I let Amanda sit there because I'm nice, but the truth is, no one ever talks Amanda out of anything once she's made up her mind. So when we pull out of the parking lot, Amanda's right behind me, like a devil over my shoulder.

She's quiet for a good stretch, but of course it doesn't last.

I can feel her breath on my neck as she leans in. "There are a lot of single women on this trip." She says it casually, like she's commenting on the weather. Which, given the number of times I've heard this refrain, or one like it, she could be doing.

"It appeals to women. Which is the whole point," I remind her. For the past year or so, Wilder Adventures has been remaking itself. We used to cater exclusively to a hard-core adventure-seeking crowd, which tended to be men, no matter how hard we tried. But suddenly, Rush Creek sprang a new hot spring, and overnight our town turned into a destination for weddings and spa-goers. It became a matter of survival for us to figure out how to market ourselves to women, couples, and families.

"Are you sure it's not those photos of you Lucy plastered all over your marketing materials? And how did she get you to take that shirtless one?"

"She snuck up on me," I growl. "She blindsided me."

Amanda snickers. "I figured." She hmms. "I think they're here for the eye candy."

"No one goes on a three-day camping trip for the eye candy," I say.

"Sure they do," Amanda says. "I mean, not everyone, but there's gotta be, statistically, say, five percent of every trip that's in it for the chance that you'll share your tent."

"Can it, Mandy-pants," I say, invoking the most forbidden of all nicknames, the one coined by her nemesis in eighth grade.

I don't even really feel guilty about it.

And Amanda, of course, is unfazed. You don't grow up the second youngest of six kids, and the only girl, without developing an extremely thick skin. "I'm just saying, Clark. If you were a little more friendly—"

"Who says I'm not friendly?" I growl.

"Grunting in a woman's general direction doesn't count as being friendly."

"I don't want to give anyone the wrong idea."

"That you're human?"

So I grunt in Amanda's general direction because anything else I say might encourage her.

For the thousandth time, I think about how, a while back, I told my brother Brody that if my sister and mom didn't lay off on the matchmaking and attempts to get me "back in the saddle," I was going to hire a fake girlfriend.

It wasn't the worst idea I've ever had.

Not that I'd ever do something like that. I don't lie, omit, or cheat, and that would be a falsehood on an epic scale.

And almost as much as actually being involved with

another woman, it would feel like a betrayal of Emma, my wife.

Dead wife.

I know it's rude and blunt to say dead, but I fucking hate the term "late" wife. She's not late. She's never coming.

Even two years later, it still feels wrong to think about another woman.

Amanda didn't get that memo, because she clears her throat, tilts her head, and eyes me in the mirror. "Jessa Olsen is pretty."

God damn it. Sometimes I think my sister can read my mind. And not in a good way.

Jessa Olsen *is* pretty.

Even though my grief over Emma's death has become a background thrum, like the sound of the ocean when you've lived near the shore forever, I still feel uncomfortable pangs of guilt and regret when I'm actively attracted to another woman.

Earlier today, I lost an internal battle and let myself take the hungry second look at Jessa I wanted. I let my eyes linger on her wavy medium-brown hair, her lush mouth—with its little bow to the upper lip. I paused there for a long moment, contemplating that mouth, then had to move on so we wouldn't end up with one too many tents on this trip. But that didn't really help, because the rest of Jessa is just as beautiful. She has clear skin, brown eyes, and just a few freckles scattered on her slightly upturned nose. A tall, slim, strong body.

Small, perfect tits! my utterly predictable dick chimes in.

"She's married," I tell Amanda.

Case closed, right?

"She's divorced." Amanda says it a little too triumphantly.

"What?" Damn. It popped out before I could stop myself. Showing curiosity about a woman around Amanda is dangerous, like leaving your phone in your back pocket when you sit on the can.

And sure enough, one of her perfectly groomed eyebrows flirts with her hairline. "Her husband cheated on her." She frowns. "It was big Rush Creek gossip for a while. Which was a whole ugly thing."

I hold up a hand. "I don't want to know." I love small town life in many ways, but there are also things I hate. Meanness. Gossip. Closed-mindedness.

She tilts her head. "You sure?"

"Positive."

I can feel Amanda's breath on my neck again. "Suffice it to say, it wasn't pretty."

I ride a wave of sympathy for Jessa—there's nothing worse than public humiliation, especially when it's unearned.

I'm lying, by the way: I want to know. I want to know the whole goddamned story. Which makes absolutely no sense. The fate of Jessa's marriage has *absolutely* nothing to do with me.

But if I'm going to find out what happened, it'll be from Jessa's own mouth.

Jessa's mouth!

The thought is accompanied by a vivid visual.

Shut up! I tell my dick.

I'll never hear that story from Jessa's mouth, because I'm never going to sit down with one of Emma's friends and have a heart-to-heart. Too fucking weird. If—and I do mean *if*—I ever date again, it's not going to be someone Emma was friends with.

Amanda takes a deep breath, which sounds like a thunderclap in my ear. Okay. I already know what's coming.

"Clark," she says, super gently.

"Don't."

"We worry about you."

"Well, quit that shit."

"You're 33. You can't just be celibate for the rest of your life."

"Who says I'm celibate? For all you know, I'm getting it on nightly."

I'm not, for anyone who's keeping track. There have been a few one-nighters over the past two years, all billed ahead of time as one-and-done. Everyone got what they signed up for, and if the experience left me numb to the core, no one had to know except me.

That's how it's going to be from now on, because I can't do it again. Love like that. Lose like that. And know that if I'd done things differently, she might still be here.

Amanda catches my eye in the mirror, and I see the moment where she realizes I'm, for real, struggling.

She bites her lip. "I'll shut up now."

"Excellent choice."

But I say it without heat. Because she's my sister, because if I know anything in life it's that she and my brothers and my mom love the shit out of me, and because, well...

Because I'm a fucking hypocrite.

Because ever since I allowed myself that second look at Jessa Olsen, I've been wishing for another one.

TRUE TO HER WORD, Amanda quits harassing me about my love life and starts in with a steady stream of chatter on how excited she is about the trip.

I'm glad someone is, because it's not me.

I'm always happy to be going into the woods, don't get me wrong, but this guided tour isn't my idea of a good time.

My idea of a good time is me and a knife, and no one knows where I am.

Instead, this trip is me, my two least survival-savvy siblings, a team of hikers with no or few wilderness skills to their names, a toilet tent, a shower tent, strings of fairy lights, bags of marshmallows, and—everything else pales in comparison—actual pillows. The Gilderness experience bills itself as "survival lite," "the perfect introduction to survival skills for people who regard toilet paper as essential to human happiness."

The concept—and the wording—were dreamed up by my brother's girlfriend, Lucy, who descended on Wilder Adventures like an avenging angel a couple of years ago and injected our modest wilderness company with new life and a shit-ton of froofy touches that, I have to admit, have seriously boosted business.

Lucy's marketing savvy is epic, and we'd have been dead meat without her, which doesn't mean I don't sometimes hate the soft stuff. But this is the fifth time we've led this particular adventure, and every time we've been able to successfully convert those very people who worship toilet paper like a lesser deity. We've gotten a whopping twenty-five percent of them to sign up for other trips.

Which, if you know marketing, is a crazy-good conversion rate. Or so Lucy tells us.

In short, you will win over more converts to camping with marshmallows and pillows than with knives and the bare forest floor.

We pull into the parking area at the trailhead. Amanda and I disembark the van and unload its contents, and everyone mingles, using the trailhead port-a-potties and introducing themselves. In a few minutes, I'll circle everyone up for a quick debrief and another round of the name game before we hit the trail. We'll hike three miles today, which is a lot for beginners but doesn't even count as a good warmup in my book.

So be it.

I'm about to holler out that everyone needs to gather 'round when I notice Jessa looks absolutely fucking miserable.

Yup, I'm looking at her again.

She's a few people away from me in the circle. Her head's ducked and her body language screams that she wants to disappear. Which I don't understand, because when we left the staging area, she was bummed that her friend was bailing, but still seemed basically game. I admired her spirit—a lot of people cancel when their friends bail out. But since then something has obviously killed her moxie.

I want to know what.

And for fuck's sake, I don't want to want that.

Even all hunched up, Jessa's prettiness and presence unsettle me, and I'm hit with a strong memory of that night at the Love for Books literacy fundraiser when I looked up and saw her. She was standing across the room, smiling and talking, eyes bright, lips red, slim body just curvy enough under her long black gown to make my own body come to life.

It was uncomfortable, like the feeling when pins and needles come back into a numb limb.

I didn't want it, or the tug I felt, the sharp desire to walk across the room and steal her attention away from whoever she was talking to.

I looked away from her and refused to look at her again.

And when she said hi to me at the food table a half hour later, I was a dick to her.

Non-redeemably.

I'm thinking about all that—Jessa smiling, talking, waking me up with her aliveness, and then how she froze when I blew her off at the food table—when I hear a voice say, "Hey, Jessa."

I raise my head to see the couple that we had to stop for. The guy is dressed in what pasty Portland hipsters think people wear in the woods, and she looks like she just came from the gym, but that's not what makes my blood freeze.

I know him.

How do I know him? I haven't put it together yet.

"Hi, Reuben," Jessa says, her voice small and tight.

Jessa knows him, too.

"I don't think you two ever officially met," Reuben says. "This is my girlfriend, Corinna." He turns to the woman beside him. She's pretty in that way that a lot of guys go for: blond, blue-eyed, busty, and polished. She's just a little too plastic for my tastes.

Jessa, standing on Reuben's other side, is a hell of a lot more beautiful. Not that anyone asked me.

I'm not the most emotionally savvy dude on the planet— after all, I spend a lot of my free time alone with a knife—but even I can tell that something seriously ugly is going on here.

The two women haven't stepped forward, not even a millimeter, to greet each other. Or even looked at each other, really. Jessa looks like she'd like the earth to swallow her. And I get the strong feeling I'm about to find out why.

Reuben turns to Corinna. "Jessa's my ex-wife."

Oh, *shit*.

That's why Jessa's mood flatlined. Because when Reuben and Corinna got on the bus, Jessa realized she was about to have to spend three days with her ex-husband and his new girlfriend. And if Amanda's intel is sound, Reuben cheated on Jessa...

I don't think you two ever officially met.

Oh, fuck. Could that guy be any more of a dick?

My hands ball into fists, and it takes everything I have not to bury one of them in his smug, asshole face.

"Nice to meet you." Jessa's voice is even smaller and tighter. And I'm not gonna lie, it hurts my chest to hear it. I know divorce isn't the same as death, not by a long shot, but that woman is *hurting*, and I'm way too familiar with that feeling.

Reuben rocks back on one foot, his arms crossing. *Now* I remember him from one of our parties. He wore a jacket with elbow patches and black-rimmed glasses. No joke.

A smug look settles on his face. "Jessa. Are you here by yourself?"

Afterwards, I'd wish I'd just punched him, because it would have been smarter than what I do next. Propelled by a force stronger than good sense and a lot faster-acting, I take a step to the side.

"She's with me."

And I drop an arm around Jessa Olsen's slim, warm shoulders.

Then I look up to discover my sister and brother staring at me like I've grown another head—

Which honestly, would have probably surprised all of us —me included—less.

3

JESSA

Three words!

Maybe Clark Wilder rations his words because he can pack a lot of disaster into a very small number of them.

A second earlier, I'd been hoping to drop through the earth's crust or be snatched away by the grim reaper or, hell, transported to a crowded New York City subway stalled out by electrical failure in the middle of a tunnel.

Anywhere but here, in short.

And then, all of a sudden, Clark's deep voice is saying, "She's with me."

His voice is at least half an octave deeper than any of the other Not Clark Wilders. It rumbles under my skin and stirs up my blood, and, bonus: He is saving me from my ugliest moment of humiliation ever.

To make matters worse, he has settled one big, hot, muscular arm around my shoulders. Its weight and heat, and the flex of his muscles, have started an instant drumbeat between my legs. And it's not just the size and weight of his arm or the man-sized hand in my peripheral vision. It's the press of his body against my side and the evergreen forest-and-Ivory-soap-and-fresh-deodorant scent of him tickling my nose.

I'm so flummoxed that I don't even think about contradicting Clark. I don't think about potential consequences or, well, anything. Instead of shaking off his arm, laughing like a loon, and saying, "Yeah, I'm here alone," I lean on Clark's shoulder, look up at him fondly, and shoot my ex a look that says, very clearly:

Top that, asshole.

It might be the first time since I found out what Reuben did that I feel like myself again.

Unfortunately, Reuben's not impressed.

He gives me a look that clearly says so, and also that he doesn't believe the charade.

Which isn't surprising, because the charade is absurd.

Clark's arm is still around my shoulder. I'm wrapped in his scent. And I'm being warmed along my right side by his body heat. He's a furnace, and I have the most overwhelming urge to turn into that heat, bury my face against his shoulder, and let myself be held.

I wonder what would happen if I did that—if he'd pull away or draw me closer?

Oh, *come on*, Jessa! He hates you!

Do guys who hate you ride in on white stallions and rescue you from dragons?

"How long have you guys been together?"

It's Corinna's voice.

The question wrenches me back to reality. It's one thing

to tell a lie as big as the one Clark has just told; it's another to double down with more made-up "facts." I look up at him, eyebrows drawn slightly together, asking, *Really? You really want to do this?*

I'm a hundred percent positive that he'll back down, but that's not what happens. Instead, he gives me a slight nod. His eyes are concerned. They're a cool gray, and they steady me. His arm tightens around my shoulder.

"What, three, four weeks, hon?" I ask him.

He nods. Looking at Clark's face at this distance is like flying too close to the sun. His cheekbones and jaw are chiseled out of stone; his nose is straight and fierce; and despite all those strong, hard lines, his mouth is so soft I think it might be begging for me to reach up and touch it.

"How did you get together?"

That's Reuben, sounding a hundred percent more doubtful than his trusting girlfriend.

How *did* we get together? My mind goes violently blank. I narrowly avoid the temptation to look up at Clark for the answer, and manage to grind out: "on another trip." It's all I can come up with.

"Not one of ours. A day hike," Clark adds. "Up Bachelor."

Reuben opens his mouth, and I know—I just *know*—that he's going to press Clark for details. And of course the two of us are going to fall apart under questioning. I know next to nothing about Clark other than the fact that he used to be married to one of my book club friends and he runs wilderness hikes.

I don't even know if he wears boxers or briefs.

For example.

I roll my eyes at myself, because now I am wondering, hard, about the answer to that question.

It's right about that moment that I finally look up and see Clark's sister Amanda and brother Kane staring at us like we're one human with two heads.

Oh, *shit*.

4

CLARK

I gently disengage my arm from Jessa's shoulder, ignore the laser beams coming from my siblings' eyes, and call, "All right people! Circle up."

Being in charge can be a really good thing. You can change the subject at any moment for any reason without having to justify yourself.

"We're going to do another round of intros, to pick up the people who joined us late. So, your name, why you chose to come on the trip, what you do when you're not on the trail."

Most of the answers are what you'd expect: Jessa Olsen, to challenge myself, wedding planner.

I'd forgotten that about her, but it makes sense: She has that feel to her, someone who could organize and motivate and keep everything running smoothly. Someone who can improvise on a moment's notice when a hotheaded mother of the bride or head waiter goes off script.

Like just now.

What the *hell* was I thinking?

I pride myself on keeping things simple, doing nothing on

impulse, and leaving plenty of distance between myself and women, except when the terms are absolutely clear.

Dropping an arm around Jessa's shoulders and telling a lie in front of my siblings does not fall into any of those categories.

I was *joking* when I told Brody that a fake relationship would solve my problems.

So *what the hell was I thinking*?

I've got to figure out how to get both of us out of this mess.

It's Reuben's turn.

"I'm Reuben Soyer. I'm the author of three published works of literary fiction, including the Cane-Lee Prize short-listed *Two Ways to Die*. I came on this trip because I wished to live deliberately."

His girlfriend smiles, tilts her head, and rests it on his shoulder.

Oh, my God. Massive prize-citing assholery aside, did he really just quote Thoreau at us?

And did it *work* for him?

Do women just drop their panties when he does that?

I cut my eyes to Jessa, who has turned slightly gray-green.

"Yeah?" I ask. "You know Thoreau's mom and sister did his laundry, right?"

A sound escapes Jessa. A smothered laugh. Feels good to make her laugh, especially when I know that with Reuben and Corinna on board, she's probably not finding much funny.

It takes us a few more minutes to finish introductions.

Amanda steams towards me, a woman on a mission. Kane's right behind her. Uh-oh.

"Clark!" Amanda trills.

I call out to our participants, "Gotta get this show on the road!"

Then before they can open their mouths to say anything, I tell Amanda and Kane, "You take the rear."

I charge to the trailhead.

Whew. Narrow escape.

What the *hell* was I thinking?

Truth is, I wasn't thinking. I was feeling. I was feeling like punching the smug look off Reuben's face, and now we're here.

I can feel my siblings' eyes boring into the back of my head as my feet find their rhythm and we eat up the first three-quarters of a mile on a steep uphill through Ponderosa pine forest.

I would feel more relaxed if I were being chased by bears.

Someone falls in beside me on the trail, and I turn to find Jessa. She's had to hike hard to catch up, and she's breathing heavily.

I try really hard not to notice the movement of her chest as she pulls in air and focus on her face instead. Her features hint at East Asian heritage and I remember that Emma once mentioned that Jessa had a Korean-American mom and a white dad.

"Hey," she says. "I just wanted to say thank you. For saving my ass—or really, my pride—back there." She cuts a little sideways look at me, a half-smile.

You're welcome seems like a dumb-ass thing to say in this situation. I struggle to figure out how to respond. I need to get myself out of this. Whatever *this* is.

What comes out is: "He's a dick."

She flinches, and I regret my choice. I could have said something softer. Kinder.

Easton, my player brother, would have known exactly the right thing to say.

Of course, Easton would also be plotting how to get into Jessa's pants, and I'm not.

"I appreciate it." Her voice is formal, stiff like her shoulders. "It redeemed what was promising to be the lowest moment of an already shitty year."

I want to ask her about the shitty year, but pretending to be her boyfriend for thirty seconds doesn't give me the right to ask personal questions, so I don't.

"Glad to help."

Damn, Clark, would it kill you to say something kind? *I know how it feels. I mean, not exactly how it feels. No one knows how anyone else feels, of course.*

Yeah, that's why I don't talk. It doesn't ever come out the way it sounds in my head, and before I know it, I've said too much.

As the trail narrows, I draw back to let her lead. She hesitates, giving me an uncertain look. "Don't you need to be up front?"

I shake my head. "No. It's fine."

Hiking behind Jessa is not a hardship. She's a strong hiker, which I really appreciate.

Don't. Look.

Don't. Look.

I look.

Wow.

She's wearing zip-on-zip-off hiking pants, and the bottoms are zipped off, which gives me a decent view of strong, tanned legs. The shorts cup her heart-shaped ass like they were molded onto it. There's the tingling in my palms again.

Want.

There's no such thing as casual sex with someone your dead wife was friends with. It's not a thing. Therefore, stop.

Just. Stop.

I look again.

Amanda crackles over the walkie-talkie—"We need a shoe-tying break back here. Slow it up for a second, Jason Momoa."

Jessa turns around, raises an eyebrow, and cracks up. I'm glad. She's feeling better; enough to laugh for real.

"Jason Momoa, huh? I can see it." She gestures vaguely in the general direction of my torso. "Jason Momoa, fresh from the barber shop."

"Is that a compliment?"

"You're kidding, right?" She gives me an incredulous look.

"I only vaguely know who Jason Momoa is."

"*Aquaman*? Khal Drogo in *Game of Thrones*?"

I shrug.

"So it's true, then? The Wilder brothers live in caves without electricity or running water, and the only movies you see are the ones you project on the walls with your hands in front of the fire."

I cough out a laugh. It feels and sounds rusty, like the creak a faucet makes when it cranks back to life after long disuse. "We're not *that* bad."

"Four words," Jessa says.

"What?"

"Nothing. You just—you don't say much."

I shrug, and for some reason, that makes a smile quirk one corner of my mouth.

She smiles in return. It's a hell of a pretty smile.

Don't. Just. Don't.

"So you look like that—" another gesture at my torso that I feel down the length of my abs, like a stroke of a hand "—from swinging from vines in the trees."

"No vines. A lot of heavy packs. And a fair number of axes and mauls."

"I'd like to see that," she mutters.

Something twinges at the base of my spine, a dark tug. Pleasant and so long-lost it's almost unfamiliar.

Amanda's voice crackles again. "OK, move it."

Jessa starts forward, but suddenly I don't want it. I don't want to see her long, strong legs or her heart-shaped ass and I definitely don't want to admire her strength and endurance and economy of motion.

I wish she hadn't come on the trip, and most of all, I wish I hadn't dropped my arm around her shoulders and laid claim.

My voice is rough and hard, like pebbles on my tongue.

"I'll go first," I tell her, brushing by, and if hurt flashes across her face, I don't let myself see it.

WE'VE REACHED CAMP, where Amanda and Kane are once again headed toward me like avengers.

"Kane," I say quickly. "Can you do the where-to-pitch-your-tent spiel?"

He gives me a dark look. "Seriously, man?"

"Gilderness looks better on you than me, dude."

He narrows his eyes.

"It pairs perfectly with your boy-next-door charm, gleaming smile, and gold highlights."

"Fuck you, dude," he says, but he's rolling his eyes and trying not to laugh.

Bonus: I have succeeded in distracting him from his curiosity about me and Jessa for long enough to make an escape.

Almost. Amanda grabs my arm. "Clark, what the—?"

"I need you on tent-pitching," I say, all business, full of shit. I mean, I *do* need her to help our clients pitch their tents, but I also need a few minutes to figure myself out before I have to answer to her.

She glares, so I point her in the direction of someone struggling to get his backpack off without toppling over. Recognizing the urgency, she sprints away.

Whew.

Kane launches into the tenting spiel, explaining how this well-used camping area is basically a larger central clearing with smaller tentable spaces positioned around it—like the spokes of a wheel.

"Pick a spot where someone pitched their tent on another trip. It'll help you leave as little trace as possible." He kneels to show the campers where the vegetation has already been trampled. "We want to demystify the woods and wilderness camping for you. To ease you into it. But we also want to start you down the path of thinking about your impact, about how you can be in the woods and leave less of a trace. How you can learn to leave nothing behind except footprints."

On a roll now—Lucy trained us well—Kane delivers the

heart of the new Wilder marketing. "The reason we call this a Gilderness experience is because it's gold-plated wilderness camping. Ultimately, we hope you'll come to feel that being close to nature is the real reward."

Okay, I was messing with him when I told him he fit the Gilderness glow, but it's also true. His boy-next-door thing *does* go perfectly with Lucy's concept for these trips. I always feel like I'm full of shit when I say that stuff, but he makes it sound good.

"If you need help, tag Clark or Amanda or me," Kane says, gesturing to the three of us. "And Clark is gonna demo how to build a shelter if you'd rather do that instead of tenting."

As a few others trail behind me, I start demo-ing the rudiments of building an A-frame shelter. A moment later, Amanda joins us, giving hands-on assistance and moral support.

"Is it possible to build one that's big enough for two?" a deep voice demands.

I look up to see that Jessa's obnoxious ex-husband and his plasti-pretty girlfriend have joined the shelter group.

And, fuck.

A shelter big enough for two.

I somehow managed to overlook the absolutely elementary fact that people who *are* together *sleep* together in the woods.

If Jessa and I sleep separately tonight, it will be abundantly clear that our ruse was bullshit.

And Reuben, author of three works of literary genius, heir to Henry David Thoreau's wilderness legacy, will definitely know it.

The big question is, why do I care so much? Our ruse *is* bullshit.

But I really, really don't want to give Reuben-the-little-shit the pleasure of realizing that Jessa is single and sad about it.

While I'm running through these thoughts in my head, Amanda pipes up. "Oh, sure, of course! Jessa and Clark slept in one together last weekend."

Whaaaaaa—?

I turn to look at her.

She gives an almost invisible shrug, raises an eyebrow at me, and smirks. Then she turns her attention back to Reuben and Blondie. "It was a little cozy, but I didn't hear them complaining. Although I'm guessing tonight they'll probably tent for a little more privacy."

She turns to me and gives me a big ol' wink for Reuben's benefit.

Pretty sure my mouth falls open.

That little—

My sister is *evil*.

At the same time, I'm kind of loving the look on Reuben's face. Like he's been smacked with a two-by-four across the midsection.

Take that, asshole!

The raw sense of victory lasts only for a second, though, because then I look up and see Jessa standing a few strides away. From the expression on her face, it's obvious she's heard every word Amanda said.

She looks like she's going to throw up, and for a second I'm positive she'll flee.

Then she squares her shoulders, pastes on a smile, and

turns to me. "Clark?" she inquires sweetly. "You ready to set up our tent? Or I'm happy to, if you're busy."

"Um," I say. "Er."

No good deed goes unpunished. Isn't that the saying?

"Go ahead, Clark," Amanda urges, generously.

"Give me a sec, Jessa?" I ask, and drag Amanda out of the clearing. When we're alone in the denser growth, I turn on my sister, stormy.

"What the *fuck* do you think you're doing?"

She pouts, innocent and wide-eyed. "I was just trying to get Reuben-the-literary-giant off Jessa's back for you."

"I can take care of Jessa myself!" I roar.

As soon as the words are out of my mouth, I can't believe I've spoken them. It's like I've just doubled down on this insanity. There *is* no taking care of Jessa myself. There *is* no Jessa and me.

This is a complete and total fiction.

And yet, I don't seem to be able to tell Amanda that.

I open and close my mouth several times without any luck.

Amanda smirks again.

We face each other, me glaring, her smirking.

"I mean," she says pointedly. "I just *assumed* that the two of you shared a tent last weekend. Since you're dating and all. And you've been together, what, three, four weeks? Since that trip where you met?"

My sister is definitely evil.

An evil genius.

And I cannot hope to beat her at any game that's essentially a battle of the wits.

I have two choices. I can 'fess up, admit that I'm full of it, and call Amanda out on her bullshit...

Or I can play along.

"Well, yeah," I say, because obviously I am the king of good decision-making today.

Amanda looks a little surprised, despite everything. She didn't believe I was going to double down again.

I feel a surge of brotherly satisfaction. Against all the odds, I think I won that round of the game.

My victory is followed by a very strong wave of panic.

Because I don't know what game we're playing.

5

JESSA

I hadn't thought all the way through to the part where two people who were dating on an adventure trip would have to spend a night together in the same tent, but I guess Amanda was a step ahead of me.

Or ten.

So much for making Amanda my friend and ally on this trip. Instead, I will have to kill her if I ever get her alone.

Although: She did kind of save me. So in the world of girl code, I'm not sure if she's my friend or my enemy.

In real life, we are acquaintances. She actually used to be in the book club I was in with Emma, but she dropped out a year before Emma died. Motherhood, marriage, and her catering business consumed her time.

I wonder what Clark is saying to her now. I'm feeling oddly guilty for having caused all this trouble, even though, in truth, none of it is my fault.

Which is itself kind of weird. I am used to being the director of my own life, the captain of my own ship, but this year has humbled me. From the disaster with my company to the mess of my divorce, it's like the universe decided to step in and put its foot down. You, Jessa Olsen, are not in charge. Brace yourself.

This is possibly just an extension of that.

Maybe I shouldn't overthink it. Maybe I should just embrace it as the adventure I was meant to have this weekend.

Clark steps out of the woods, looking like a Viking crossed with a thunderstorm. Despite myself, I draw back, a little shivery at his fierceness. You would not want to meet him in a dark alley (or the dark woods).

And yet my body thinks that's a very good idea. Clark in the dark woods. In a tent. At night. Just the two of us.

Embrace it.

He gives me a look that is almost a glare. Guess he's not having the same fond thoughts.

"It's not my fault," I tell him.

Something that might be a smile cracks the ferocity of his expression, and he nods. Not like a whole nod. One of those half nods that really alpha men give when they greet you on the street. All the Wilders are experts at The Nod.

"My sister is a force of nature," Clark says gruffly. Seven words. We're definitely into full-sentence territory now.

"She really is."

I'd like to be her friend, actually. After I kill her.

"Look," he says, still gruff. "You don't have to spend a night in a tent with a strange man."

I shrug. "You're not *that* strange. Apart from the vine swinging, and I can get behind that if it leads to arm-toning like yours."

He snorts. Even though it's not quite a real laugh, it still tugs in my low belly. I don't think Clark Wilder laughs much, and there's something pretty fantastic about eking one out of him.

I wonder how it would feel to make Clark Wilder laugh out loud.

Or groan with pleasure?

Aaand, enough of that.

He frowns. "We can set up the tent, but I'll crawl out after we go in and sleep somewhere else."

"You don't have to do that."

"I'm not spending the night in the same tent with you," he says flatly.

Okay, that's not flattering. I'm over here thinking about how sleeping in a tent with Clark Wilder might be the closest I've been to orgasm in a year, and he's trying to wiggle out of being in an enclosed space with me.

"Look," I say, just so we're totally on the same page. "I get it. This is super weird. I'm Emma's friend. You're still grieving. Just so you know, I would never try to—" Fuck, why is being human so hard? "—put the moves on you or anything."

He looks startled, like the idea had never crossed his mind. "I didn't think that."

"We don't have to go through with this at all. I'm sure we can come up with an excuse. I have terrible, um, beard allergies."

He gives me an incredulous look.

"It's a thing!" I insist.

"I'm hypoallergenic," he says, which makes me snicker. The corner of his mouth tips up. It's a thing of beauty. Who knew? Clark Wilder has a sense of humor.

Which kind of sucks, because now it's even more of a

bummer that the idea of spending the night in a tent with me is such a hardship for him.

"Okay, fine, so we'll tell them I can't sleep when you're snoring."

"I don't snore."

"You're missing the point!" I say. "We can get out of this without you having to marine crawl through underbrush at midnight."

He shakes his head. "No. You're missing the point. We have to at least get into the tent together at bedtime. I can't give Amanda the satisfaction of admitting it was a lie." He scowls. "She knows I'm full of it and she's dying for the moment when I have to admit it. You should have seen her just now. She was so sure I'd blink after she said that thing to Reuben."

I raise my eyebrows. "Wait a second. Are you saying you'd pretend to sleep in a tent with me just so you don't have to back down from a pissing contest with your sister?"

"She fights mean," he says simply. His gaze leaves mine and finds a spot slightly over my head. Something goes blank behind his eyes. "But also, Emma would kill me if I backed out on you now."

Something knots in my chest. I want him to sleep in the tent. But I don't want him to do it just because he wants to win a fight with his sister. And even more than that, I *really* don't want him to do it because his dead wife would have wanted him to.

"Hand me your tent bag." He holds out one big, thick-fingered hand, and my sex drive responds with a white flag.

Obviously, it's conversation over, and I'm spending the

night in a tent with a guy who, at best, doesn't hate me as much as I thought.

A moment later, Jason Momoa is pitching my tent.

God, look at those arms. He's wearing a brown base layer which clings to him like super-hero skin, throwing every curve and plane into sharp relief. I probably couldn't wrap both my hands around his bicep. And do men's forearms have extra parts, like tendons and muscle and stuff, that we don't even have? I can't take my eyes off those arms.

He gets the tent up in seconds flat. Like, I'm still struggling to extricate the stakes from the little tie-bag they're in, and he's calling for them. I fumble, do a quick save, and hand them to him, and he stakes down the tent. I watch him wield a rock like a hammer and think about that disturbing line between sexy and cave man, and how most women I know walk it like a tightrope. (Or would that be climb it like a tree?) Clark has that super-hot economy-of-motion vibe going on. Like, he doesn't move a muscle until it's time, and then it's all compact, pent-up power.

Nnnngh.

Just then, something flutters in my peripheral vision. I turn and discover that the top flap of my backpack is wiggling wildly, like it has suddenly developed a life of its own. I can't help it, I let out a shriek and grab onto the nearest thing I can —which happens to be Clark. One moment I'm a perfectly sensible human, the next I'm a koala on Clark's big arm.

Big, hard, very muscular arm.

He looks down at me, and something ripples across his face. It might be amusement—or (my body says) it might be something else.

Whatever it is lasts only a split second and is gone. Then

he very gently peels me off his arm, strides to my pack, and tips it sideways, dislodging a chipmunk, which scolds us before scurrying into the woods.

"Oh," I say, feeling my face burn bright red. "Chipmunk."

"Yup," he says.

He retrieves the rock and goes back to staking my tent.

I can still feel the heat and textures—smooth skin, rough hair—of his arm under my hands.

Tonight, I'm going to crawl into a tent with this guy. And yes, he's going to crawl out again at some point, but the most absurd part is, I don't want him to.

THE WILDERS HAVE this glamping thing down to a science.

We're in the middle of the wilderness, so far from civilization that you can't hear a single man-made noise except the ones we've brought with us. And yet, we have all the creature comforts.

They set up a shower tent and a toilet tent and string battery-operated fairy lights between them. They pass out Wilder-branded mosquito netting and Wilder-branded pillows to all their participants. They hand around pre-rationed TP squares (something about a lesson Brody learned?), attached to a little guide to toileting in the woods: "Toileters who squat, keep your tush downhill from your boots," it advises, and has a tear-out card you can use to send away for a free Wilder Adventures t-shirt (and also request more information about survival trips).

I know from word-around-town that this is the brilliant masterwork of Lucy Spiro, Gabe Wilder's girlfriend. I wish like hell my wedding business had enough cash flow to pull her in for a couple of hours of marketing consulting. The business is still reeling from a blow it took last year, and it could use some outside support so when I leave this fall it's in the best possible shape. But the money's just not there.

Amanda invites my tripmates to learn camp stove cooking with her, the owner of Around the Table catering. "This is the Around the Campfire division," she beams at everyone. "How to make tastier meals in the woods."

I start to follow her, but before I can establish a position in the front ring of observers, we're joined by Reuben and Corinna. Holding hands. And Reuben is already talking.

"When I was doing research for my novel—the short-listed prize winner *Forest Floor*—I actually did all my cooking over a camp stove just like that one for a whole month," Reuben tells Amanda.

"Did you?" she asks cheerfully.

"The trickiest thing is a sauce béarnaise."

In my defense, I swear he was not like this when I met him or when I accepted his marriage proposal. He has become a bigger dick with every book he publishes.

"Haven't tried that." Amanda's tone's still friendly.

"If you haven't cooked a sauce béarnaise over a camp stove, you haven't really cooked over a camp stove," Reuben says, beaming and nodding like he's just said something she'll totally agree with.

Amanda, to her credit, smiles pleasantly. Or—if I'm not mistaken—slightly dangerously.

Once she has four burners going, she puts one of my tripmates in charge of stirring and keeping the gas adjusted right. Then she surprises me by drifting to my side.

"You *were married* to that guy," Amanda says. "The author. Sorry, the prize-winning author."

"Uh, yeah?"

She raises her eyebrows. "I have several questions. The biggest of which is, Is he short-listed all over?"

I crack up. "A woman never kisses and tells."

She smiles at me. "He's a piece of work. How'd you keep from killing him?"

I sigh, weight settling into my chest. "That isn't really the question. The real question is, why didn't I realize sooner I should have wanted to? You know how when you're in love with someone, you ignore their most aggravating traits?"

Amanda smiles. "I do, actually."

Her smile tells me that whoever's traits aggravate her, she still really loves him.

"I didn't realize he was an asshole until—" I hesitate. "Until I was the direct object of his awfulness. He was the biggest mistake of my life."

Amanda's warm gray eyes search my face. I must look stricken, because she says, "You wouldn't be the first woman to fall for an asshole, and you won't be the last." She cocks her head. "Although I guess in this case we could hope Corinna's the last. For the sake of women everywhere."

We both peer over in Reuben and Corinna's direction. Reuben is holding forth on something to do with the food, and Corinna is listening raptly.

I used to be like that. I've always been a sucker for the intense, self-confident type. That's probably why I fell for Reuben, because even if he wasn't actually that deep, he was good at playing the part of the brooding literary artiste.

She puts a hand on my shoulder. "So. You're dating my

brother, huh?"

Ack! Trap!

"Nevermind, don't answer that," she says. "You have a fifth amendment right not to self-incriminate." She pauses, running a hand through her dark brown hair. She has a feminine version of the Wilder face—diamond-saw cheekbones and deep-set eyes and a soft mouth. "So, you, uh, still in the old book club?"

I shake my head. "It broke up after Emma died."

"You in one now?"

I nod. "Just joined. But I'm not loving it. There's a mean girl in it. She's a terror. She has this teeny-tiny dog, Chicklet—"

"Ohhh," Amanda says. "Yes. We all know Chicklet. Brody once had to dive into a lake on a boating trip to rescue Chicklet. And then Jennifer destroyed Brody in online reviews. Long story. Happy ending. You'll hear it soon enough, since you're *dating Clark*." She gives me a pointed look.

Ack again! She knows it's bullshit. Obviously.

"Actually," she says, the look growing even more pointed, "You can ask him to tell you about it. Tonight. *In your tent*."

Now would be an excellent time for me to own up to the fact that Clark and I are nothing to each other besides people who once bumped heads hard enough to cause a minor concussion. And yet I don't. If Clark didn't want Amanda to know he was bullshitting her, it's not my place to out him.

He did, after all, save my ass earlier today—or at least my pride.

"I'll do that."

She gives me a look that I'm pretty sure is fifty percent incredulity and fifty percent admiration. Then she jumps.

"Oh, *shit*, I forgot I was cooking. Sorry to run off." She tips her head to indicate Reuben. "You gonna be okay?"

"Yup."

She hustles back to the cookstove, leaving me with my own thoughts. Which are mostly: *Oh, my God, what have I done?*

And why do I keep doing it?

A voice rumbles over my nerve endings. "Anyone who wants to see a fire-starting demonstration, I'm doing one over here."

Since I'm not going back to where Reuben is once again manstructing Amanda, I head to the demonstration. Not because every little hair on my body stood up and leaned towards the sound of that deep voice. Not at all.

And I get a front row seat to Clark.

He's pushed up the sleeves of his base layer to reveal the bare tanned skin and dark gold hair of his forearms.

He's kneeling, his thick tree-trunk thighs straining the fabric of his hiking pants.

Both of his thick, calloused hands are around a stick, and he's using those hands to twirl the stick in a shallow indentation as he narrates. His forearms flex and contract.

Words are coming out of his mouth, but all I hear is "friction" "heat" "spark."

It's really all I need to hear. Any more, and I'd do the combusting.

"I have an ember now," Clark says, and kneels lower, his mouth pursing to form a kiss, and blows gently as he adds small bits of bark and grass.

He's coaxing it into flame.

I should know.

6

CLARK

This tent is small. Like so fucking small.

Oh God, it's so small.

The tent, that is. The tent is the only thing that's small, or that stands the slightest chance of ever being small, again.

Aside from those few no-strings one-nighters I've had, I haven't been this close to a woman for a sustained period of time since…

Since Emma.

She smells SO GOOD.

How is that even possible? She did the same hike I did. But she still manages to give off the scent of flowers and baked goods.

Also, from time to time she moves, and her hair swishes across the nylon of the tent, and just the sound of it is enough to make me crazy.

And as if all of that is not enough, when she grabbed my arm and latched on like a baby monkey to its mother, I could feel the softness of her breasts, a memory I am not likely to forget any time soon.

Do they use sexual deprivation as a form of torture to get prisoners to talk?

They should.

"Clark," Jessa whispers.

My throat closes, dark and tight. "Yeah?"

"Do you think you could, um, safely leave now?"

I can't blame her for asking this question. We've been awkwardly sitting in here, curled up in opposite corners of the tent, silently staring at each other and listening like hawks for the sounds outside to die down. Still, I want to do the opposite of leaving.

I want to bury my face where that smell is most concentrated and use my tongue to make her gasp.

She wants me to get the hell out of here so she can sleep.

And that's exactly what I should do.

Straining my ears, I hear nothing but forest sounds.

"I'll give it a shot," I tell her.

"Good luck," she whispers back.

As quietly as I can, I unzip the tent and, grabbing my sleeping bag, ease myself out. I deliberately leave my headlamp off, for stealth. I don't marine crawl, because that would be absurd, but I do move as silently as possible, drawing on old army training. I think there's a single empty tenting area directly across the wheel-shaped area from us.

Voices drift to me from the central clearing.

And not just any voices. As I get closer, I can see that it's Reuben and Corinna, whispering and giggling. They've zipped their sleeping bags together and are lying under the stars, staring up. As I watch, they roll toward each other, and...

Oh. Wow. No way. They're not actually going to...

The bag humps up and I turn away, because ugh.

They are.

I close my eyes in a vain hope that it will also somehow shut out Corinna's little gasping noises, but no luck.

Maybe they're so into each other that I could sneak by them? I take another careful step, and something crackles underfoot.

So much for training.

The heaving sleeping bag mound stills. "What was that?" Reuben stage whispers. Like all little shits, he's wound way too tight.

"I didn't hear anything," Corinna purrs.

"Listen!"

Okay, so I'm not going through the center of the wheel. I'll head back past our tent and skirt the outside edge of the camping areas. I glide slowly in the other direction.

"Did you hear that?" Reuben's voice drifts toward me from behind.

"No," Corinna says. "Get that big thing back over here."

Double ugh. I hope Jessa can't hear them.

I hurry away from them. I wind back past the tent and start my trip around what I think is the outside of the circle of tenting areas. It's dark, though, and I can't have a light on or someone will see me and it'll get back to Kane or Amanda or Reuben.

I nearly trip over something in the dark.

"Jesus, Clark! Watch your step." A flashlight comes on,

momentarily blinding me. I put up both hands. The light goes off.

The voice is Kane's. A moment later, the light comes back on, turned away from me, and I can see him, sprawled out in his sleeping bag on a folded-up tarp. He glares up at me. "Where are you going?"

I calculate my situation with a split second thought. Kane and Amanda are tight. Whatever I say to Kane will get back to Amanda. Normally my brothers are my allies against the world, but that doesn't apply in this situation. So I do what any self-respecting Wilder would do. I flat-out lie. "Taking a leak."

Even in the dark, I can see his eyebrows go up. "With your sleeping bag in your arms?"

"I, uh—there was a spider in it. I'm shaking it out."

"Uh-huh," Kane says. "Did it get too cozy in the tent for you, Romeo?"

"Shut up."

"As you wish," Kane says, Westley-in-Princess-Bride style.

"I can still beat you up," I remind him.

"Yeah, but if you do, Gabe will kick your ass."

I sigh. He chuckles.

"Sleep tight," I tell him. I take another tack into the woods, where I'm obliged to take a piss for the sake of the charade. It's more of a trickle.

"Sounds like it was urgent," Kane says dryly from the darkness.

"Fuck you."

Another chuckle.

I tuck myself away and ponder my options. If I looped

back around the tent and seemed to go inside, then I could go the other direction.

I start off with that intention, but I'm barely past the tent when I see a light. I slow down, approaching as silently as I can.

It's an e-reader.

Amanda's e-reader.

She deliberately planted herself on one side of our tent and Kane on the other, so I wouldn't be able to sneak out without one of them noting it.

Evil genius, like I said.

In a war, I would rather take on any—or even all—of my brothers than Amanda. She's just altogether too crafty. In an Amanda vs. The Brothers battle, she could win solo.

Come to think of it, she spent her childhood perfecting that art.

Only-girls in families of brothers are tough humans.

"Hey, Clark," Amanda stage whispers.

"Hey, Amanda," I woods-whisper back. "Just headed back to my tent."

"Mmm-hmm," she purrs.

Wow, she's frustrating. I drop my sleeping bag and head to her side.

"No e-readers on the trip," I say in my best gruff leader voice. "I need to confiscate that." I reach my hand down and grab it.

She just smiles at me.

Oh, that's not good. Not good at all.

"Go ahead," she says. "Confiscate it. And I'll tell mom that you're dating Jessa."

Oh, *shit*.

I give her the e-reader back.

"Love you, big bro."

"You're evil."

"But you love me anyway."

"I do," I admit. "I don't know why, but I do."

I scoop up my sleeping bag and accept my fate. I have to go back to Jessa's tent unless I want to fess up.

When I unzip the tent and let myself back in, things have shifted somewhat. Jessa is in her sleeping bag, lying down. I hear her quiet breathing. She couldn't have fallen asleep yet, could she?

"Jessa?" I murmur.

"Mmm?"

"Never mind. Go back to sleep."

"You're back?"

"Kane is on one side. Amanda's on the other. Reuben and Corinna are in the clearing."

"Well, hell," she says. "It's like an FBI stakeout."

I smile. "Yeah. Have to wait for them to fall asleep."

"You mind if I sleep?"

"Nah. Go ahead. I'll just stay in here till everyone conks out."

I edge back to my corner of the tent. She curls up and turns away from me. We're quiet.

Sounds slide into the tent. Reuben and Corinna's noises. Face sucking and quiet moans, murmurs and laughs.

That bastard.

I *really* hope Jessa isn't listening. Or if she is, that she can't recognize Reuben's weird groaning noises.

No such luck, though. "Can't they just—?" Her voice is

muffled by her sleeping bag. "I mean, does he have any decency?"

"Doesn't seem like it."

I don't want Jessa to have to listen to the sounds of her ex-husband and his new girlfriend making love under the stars. I'm not good at making conversation, but desperate times call for desperate measures. I need to distract her.

"I've made this worse. Instead of helping."

Her answer comes back, quick and firm. "No. You couldn't have foreseen. Unintended consequences." She struggles to a sitting position, keeping the sleeping bag tucked around her. There's a slant of moonlight through the open flap of the tent, and it touches her face, bouncing off the sweet curve of her cheek. She's so pretty. For a second, I have to bite back the urge to touch the light where it touches her.

The impulse drags me back to what a dumbass idea this all was.

I sigh. "If I'd thought about it for three seconds I probably could have guessed that pretending to be your date for this trip would have some consequences. I just didn't think."

"Yeah. Well. What I'm saying is, I'm grateful you didn't, even if this is—" She doesn't finish the sentence.

"Weird? Awkward?"

"I mean, yeah? Both? But also kind of hilarious. I keep wanting to burst out laughing. Is it crazy to say I'm having fun?"

It's funny, but until she says it, I hadn't realized it was true. The feeling in my chest, a kind of giddy wave, is the long-forgotten sensation of having a good time.

"And the best part is, it's fun at Reuben's expense," Jessa adds.

It gets quiet again, and we both distinctly hear Corinna say, "Harder, Rube."

"Jesus," Jessa whispers.

"I'm sorry," I whisper back.

"Ask me something. Anything. I need to not listen."

I remember how desperate I was not to think or feel in the days after Emma died. Without planning, I ask, "What happened? To your marriage?" And then, "Shit. That's probably not the distraction you were hoping for."

"No. I don't mind. It's better than listening to them. What happened was, I thought everything was fine. Like, really fine. I was happy, he was happy, we were happy together. And then my best friend, Imani, called me up. She wanted to know if I'd read his new book. I hadn't. Because I hated the first two. He called them novels, but he stole everything from real life. Only he made himself taller, better looking, and more competent."

"Why is that not surprising?"

Jessa smiles, a quick white gleam in the dark. Then the smile disappears. "I read it. The third book." Her voice gets smaller. I can tell we're getting to the part of the story I'm going to hate. "It's just like the first two. Obviously autobiographical. To the point where he's married to this woman who is half Korean-American and half white, and she's an event planner, although it's corporate events, not weddings—"

"What the fuck?" I demand. "At least *try* to pretend."

"Right? Anyway, I keep reading, even though I'm getting increasingly uncomfortable, because the wife character is kind of an ice queen. She's just—self-contained. He can't get through to her. She's slow to warm up, and he's this creative type with big feelings—"

"You know that's just bullshit, right?" I growl. "He's just a big fucking baby who can't actually write fiction." I want to say more, to build her up with the fact she's pretty and smart and funny, but the truth is, I don't know her that well and I don't want her to feel like I'm just blowing smoke up her ass. So I keep it simple. "I'm sorry. That really sucks."

"That's not even the bad part."

"Wait. How is that not the bad part? He published a book where he made you into an ice queen and himself into the hero!"

She looks away. I think maybe she's not going to answer at all. Then she looks back, bites her lip, and says, "In the book, he has an affair."

"Oh, *shit*."

Jessa hunches down a little. Her head almost disappears into the turtle shell of her sleeping bag.

Pretty sure I know what's coming, and I hate the fuck out of it.

"That's how I found out Reuben was sleeping with Corinna," Jessa says. "About ten weeks *after* everyone else found out."

7

JESSA

I stop there and let Clark take it in. I will say this for Reuben: He left me with such a good story to tell. No one hears that story without feeling sorry for me. No one says, "Oh, that poor guy. I bet he couldn't think of any better way to tell you he wanted to end the marriage."

Not that I tell a lot of people.

Not that I *need* to tell a lot of people. I'm sure they all read Reuben's novel. Sometimes, when people ask me what happened to my marriage, I'm tempted to just hand them the book.

Maybe I should start doing that.

"Jesus, Jessa!" Clark says. "What a bastard!"

There's something about this big lug of a guy, bearded and fierce, and his anger and his sympathy, that makes my eyes fill with tears again.

"Yeah. Everyone I knew read it, and no one told me about it. I guess they didn't know how. You can't blame them. I mean, how do you tell someone her husband cheated on her and wrote about it in a book? It's not something Emily Post had much to say about."

"That... *fucker*," Clark growls. "That absolute fucking piece of useless shit."

Bearded, fierce, and ragingly pissed on my behalf.

It's kind of hot.

He could kill Reuben pretty easily.

Is it wrong that I sort of hope Reuben does something to set him off and I get to see him die at Clark's hands?

Of course it's fucking wrong, Jessa. What on God's green earth have you been smoking?

But probably kind of human, too, I allow myself.

Clark is shaking his head. With that thick hair and beard, he's as beautiful as a lion. "I can't believe—"

"No one can," I say. "On the plus side, I went from loving him to hating him pretty fast."

We're both quiet for a moment, and I'm sure we're thinking the same thing. There are definitely multiple ways to lose someone. The man I loved turned out not to be the man I thought he was, and that sucked in one kind of way. And the woman Clark loved—

Well, she stayed the woman he loved and he lost her completely.

I can tell he's thinking about her, too, because he ducks his head.

And now Emma's in the tent with us.

It's a good reminder that even though I find him insanely attractive, I can't act on it. We're both bruised and battered, and on top of that, there's girl code. I'm pretty sure girl code isn't *till death do us part*, but forever. You don't mess around with your friend's widower, especially if you know you're kind of a disaster when it comes to sex, love, and everything that goes with.

If I screwed him over by mistake, I'd not only know I'd hurt a good man, but I'd have to answer to a rage-y ghost.

Time for a subject change. "So did you just get into the wilderness thing because it was the family business?"

The lion shakes his head again, this time like he's sloughing off whatever dark thoughts I'd conjured into the tent. "Actually, no. I thought I wasn't going to do it. My dad died six months before 9/11, when I was twelve, and after 9/11 I knew I wanted to serve, at least for a while. I ended up going to college the Army ROTC route, and then doing my active service."

"So you learned survival the hard way."

He nods. "It's everyday reality in Afghanistan." He's quiet for a moment, and I wonder about what followed him home. Emma might not be the only ghost in his world.

His eyes come back to mine. "Anyway, Gabe eventually begged me to come back, so I did. I stayed in the reserves for a while, then left. Now I do the family business, and wilderness rescue, too, when I'm needed."

"I can totally see that. Do you miss being a soldier?"

His answer comes quickly. "No. I like working with my brothers. Love my family."

I like how easily he says it. This total mountain man—big, rough, hyper-competent, and completely in touch with his love for his people.

I get it, Emma. I totally get it.

I'm really sleepy, and I've gradually drifted into the sleeping bag so I'm more or less lying down. He's still sitting up—he must be exhausted and cold by now.

"I should—"

He gestures outside.

"Do you want to just lie down?" I ask him.

"I should get out of here."

Our eyes meet. There's something soft and vulnerable in his. He does not look like a predator. And sometimes you just have to follow your instincts.

"I trust you," I tell him.

His expression gets even softer.

"Maybe I shouldn't, but I do. I mean, let's face it, I could scream and your sister and brother would be in here in three seconds."

His mouth quirks. "That's not trust. That's a backup plan."

"But I do. Trust you."

He raises an eyebrow.

"C'mon, Clark. Even if you sleep out there, you'll have to come back in here before everyone wakes up or you'll be right back where you started."

"True," he admits.

"I'll stay on my side of the tent."

He raises his eyebrows. "You're not the one I'm worried about."

Oh. Really? Does that mean he's worried about *him* not staying on his side?

Is he *flirting*?

That probably means he doesn't hate me. Possibly he never hated me.

"We could put a pack between us," he suggests.

I shake my head. "We'll be fine."

He peruses my face carefully, giving me one more chance to change my mind. When I don't, he spreads his sleeping bag out—being careful to keep his hands away from my body.

Those big hands.

I would not mind if he put them closer to my body.

On my body.

I shiver, and not from the cold.

We're stretched out side by side now. There's a careful distance between us. I wriggle until my body touches my side of the tent, to make the distance bigger. So he'll feel more comfortable, not because I need more space between us.

"You don't want to be touching the side of the tent. Or you'll end up damp from the dew."

I back off a fraction, and we lie there in silence. I can feel the whole length of him like he's giving off a heat signature I know by heart. I wonder if he feels it too, the supercharged space between us.

He coughs. "I'll let you go to sleep now."

"You don't have to. I'll fall asleep right in the middle of my own sentence."

"You can talk yourself to sleep?"

"Mmm-hmm."

He chuckles. "Okay. If you say so."

Just then, with the worst timing on earth, I hear another distinct, unmistakable Reuben grunt.

"Shit," Clark says quietly.

"Just ask me something. Anything."

I meant what I said about falling asleep while I'm talking. As long as I don't have to listen to Reuben pound his girlfriend, I'll be fine.

He's quiet for another moment, then asks, "Is your family in Rush Creek? Or nearby?"

"My parents are in Portland now, but I grew up on the East Coast—outside of Philly—then went to college in Eugene. University of Oregon. My mom's parents came to the U.S. from South Korea in the early 1960s. My mom was born and raised in Philly." I pause, then continue. "My father's white—German, British, Irish, whatever. They met in college and fell in love. I have two siblings I fought with and who I love."

"Brothers? Sisters?"

"A sister and a non-binary sibling."

"Cool. Are your sibs on the East Coast? Or out here?"

I guess Clark has a comfort level with gender fluidity, because he didn't balk at switching from gendered to non-gendered language, and he didn't ask, as most people do, what Madison's assigned birth sex was. I don't mind helping people figure out how to talk about Madison, but I always appreciate it when I don't have to.

"Courtney's in the Peace Corp in Ghana. Madison lives with their boyfriend near my parents outside Philly. They're having a baby in mid-October." I think I slur some of the words. I'm so sleepy. *I'm moving back East to be near Mad and Ferris and help with the baby.* I think it, but don't say it, because I'm getting too drowsy to form words.

"Do you get along well with both your sibs now that you're adults?"

I try to answer, but somewhere in the middle of the sentence, I drift off.

8

CLARK

In the dream, I'm kissing a woman, my body on top of hers. We're fully dressed, but I can feel her soft curves, the firm press of her hip and pubic bones. Our movements are slow—underwater slow—and intensely hot, the kisses deep, the rocking of our bodies synced. It's that perfect blend of urgent and go-all-night. If you focus, if you ride it, you *could* go all night, the two of you closer and closer until you fall into orgasm.

I know the woman under me isn't Emma, but I don't let myself think about that. Whoever it is, I care about her. I feel connected to her. And I've missed this feeling so fucking much. More than the sex. Much more.

I wake up on the brink of coming, hard as a rock, to find myself wrapped around Jessa. Not on her, thankfully, but spooning her so tight that if she were awake—which blessedly, I'm pretty sure she isn't—she'd feel my erection through two layers of sleeping bag.

Jesus, Clark, you animal! I chastise myself, yanking myself away from her as quickly as I can without waking her. I hurriedly extract myself from my sleeping bag, jam my feet into boots, hastily untie a white rag from my pack, and crawl out of the tent. The air is cool on my flushed face, my body so hard it hurts. Fuck. I stand for a moment, trying to orient myself; the last thing I want is to make a mad dash into the woods and get lost. Super embarrassing if the trip leader has to be rescued.

Also, I still don't want to wake up my siblings. As much as I didn't want to reveal the truth—that Jessa and I aren't really together—I want less to reveal this new truth: That I would have fucked her into next week if she'd been awake and willing.

I hustle out of the tent, into the woods, away from my sleeping siblings. I'm tearing strips off the rag I grabbed as I walk, tying a chain of white cloth flags on trees as I venture further into the woods. All I want is to get away. Away from having broken Jessa's trust, away from the scent of her, still filling my nose, and away from how fucking horny I am.

I can't, though. I can't get away from how aroused I am. It's demanding all my attention, gripping the base of my spine, like a fist around—

Clark, don't you—

Don't you *dare*.

But I do dare. I stop where I am, take another survey of my surroundings, make sure I'm alone. I push my sweatpants down, freeing myself. I'm so hard it hurts, the skin swollen and shiny over the bare, cut head of my cock. It takes just a few strokes, fist tight, before I'm coming, spilling on the ground, huffing out frustration and relief and a whole lot of shame.

I kneel, dig, and clean up—myself and the forest—the best I can.

Then I stand up and lean against a tree.

Holy shit.

I haven't felt like that—urgent, mindless—in years.

And there's a strange, blissful peace in its aftermath—much more than any short-lived peace I've been able to get from my few quick, casual encounters.

There's shame, though, too. For being so out of control.

I want to apologize to everyone: Emma, Jessa, the woods, because I don't think that counts as leave-no-trace.

Have to look that one up when I get back to civilization.

I push myself to standing. The sky has lightened, and I realize, suddenly, that I've woken up just before the sunrise, which puts the time around 4:45 am. We're a short hike from an overlook, and I decide that since I'm awake, with damn near no chance of falling back to sleep, I might as well take a peek.

Sunrise comes on slowly, blooming orange, red, purple, peach, and I stand there a long time, watching it, trying to feel the edges of my shame around the excitement that I can't quite push away.

9
―――
JESSA

"Hey."

It's taken me all morning and all of my strength and endurance to catch up with Clark at the front of the hiking line. Yesterday it was easier to keep up with him. Today, I'm pretty sure he's charging ahead on purpose.

He probably feels bad about the middle-of-the-night groping.

I'm not sure how I feel about the middle-of-the-night groping.

Last night, I woke up in the darkest part of the night with Clark spooning me. Tightly.

A couple of weeks ago, I went to a sex toy party hosted by Brody Wilder's girlfriend, Rachel Perez, and she showed us a whole bunch of dildos. All different sizes—five, six, seven, eight inches. She talked a bunch about the whole "size matters" v. "it's not the size of the boat, it's the motion of the ocean," thing. Her position ("No pun intended!" she bubbled.) was that there's no perfect size, just the size that works for you. When the eight-inch dildo came around the circle and landed in my palm, I looked at it thought, *Nope. Too much.*

But last night, with eight (or more) inches pressing against me through two sleeping bags, I was *not* thinking, *Nope.*

I was thinking, *Yes.*

Maybe it was sexual deprivation. I haven't slept with anyone since Reuben, and (a sign which I should have attended to, but didn't), Reuben and I didn't have much sex the last six months of our marriage. So it's been almost eighteen months since I had an orgasm that wasn't delivered by vibrator.

Or maybe it was the strange circumstances of our situation. Clark's unexpected rescue of me, his continued willingness to go to bat to keep my pride intact. The way he talked over the sex sounds outside our tent, so I wouldn't have to listen to Reuben spend himself into the woman he'd cheated on me with.

Or maybe it was the strange vulnerability I felt after telling Clark about what Reuben did to me, or how hurt and angry he got on my behalf.

Whatever it was, the press of Clark's hard cock against my ass made me think, *Yes.*

I had to marshal all my self-control not to wriggle back against him. He was definitely asleep; I could hear the deep steady thrum of his breathing.

I knew the exact moment when he woke up, too. He froze. His breath stopped. His whole body—not just my new favorite part of it—went rigid. And he backed himself up slowly, like a mammoth piece of construction equipment, minus the beeping.

He left the tent in a hurry and for a good long time. When he came back, he settled himself as far away from me as humanly possible.

But I could still smell him. Juniper, sage, resin—like fresh-cut brush. Butterscotch and vanilla, the smells of Ponderosa pine bark.

He smells like the forest, like the Pacific Northwest.

I can smell it as we hike together in silence now, along with the slight tang of sweat, which only improves the olfactory experience.

His chin is down a bit, and he hasn't looked at me, not once.

I don't want him to feel bad about the groping. It was sleep-groping and doesn't mean anything. And the only way to make sure it doesn't become a thing is to bring it out into the open air.

So now that I've managed to power up beside him, I dive right into that topic, before he can escape or evade.

"It's not a big deal," I say.

He makes a choked noise. "Um, what?"

Oh. Don't make me say it. Please don't make me say it.

He's going to make me say it.

But he doesn't make me say it. He asks, very quietly, "You were awake? When I—mmm—accidentally—?" He casts a sideways glance my direction.

I wrinkle my nose, an apologetic *yes*.

"Oh, God, Jessa, ugh. I'm so sorry!"

"It's not a big deal," I repeat. "You were asleep. I woke up, I knew you were asleep, I don't in any way hold you responsible."

"Still!"

"I didn't—" I'm blushing. But the poor guy! I don't want him to beat himself up for middle-of-the-night wood. (*Beat himself off?* a naughty little voice in my head chimes in, and the resulting mental picture makes my breath catch.) "I didn't mind."

I was trying to make it sound cool and nonchalant, but not gonna lie, it comes out breathy and suggestive.

Whoops.

There's a long silence from beside me. Just the two of us, both breathing hard. Like we would if we were—

Jessa! I chastise myself.

"Well," Clark says. He clears his throat. Then, again. "Tonight, I should sleep somewhere else." His gaze hangs on my face for a moment, his eyes dark and curious. I can't tell if he's saying that's what he wants, or asking if it's what I want. And I can't imagine what question I would ask to figure it out.

Clark stops abruptly. For a second, I think it's to force the issue, but then I realize his stopping has nothing to do with our conversation. "Hold up!" he calls over my head and down the line of hikers. "Overlook here."

He points, and we follow a side trail to a beautiful overlook, a view of a river valley far below, the white and aqua water carving a canyon through pale red rock and dark green trees.

Clark heaves his pack down, says, "Bio break," and vanishes.

We're back to two words at a time.

I guess I scared him.

Or he scared himself.

I rest my own pack on a high rock beside me and stare out at the gorgeous view.

It's probably good that he got scared off, because what did I think was going to happen? That we would temporarily put aside the intersection point in our lives—Emma—and have a tumble in the tent, then walk away?

Nah. That was never gonna happen.

Even if my body is fired up along every nerve ending, wanting to be close to him and those eight inches again.

The smart thing to do would be to stage a breakup today. We've just been together a couple of weeks, and we realized this isn't really right for us.

"Hey, Jessa!"

Reuben has come up beside me. Seriously? The guy is everywhere I need him not to be.

I look around for Corinna. She's sitting beside Kane on a big flat rock, pointing at something in the distance.

"How are you liking the Gilderness experience?" he asks, friendly as can be, like he never put me in a book and exposed me to the world.

Well. Two can play at that game.

"Loving it," I say. "So much fun."

"So. You and Conan, huh?"

I bite down on a strong, reflexive desire to tell him to fuck himself. "Yup."

"I wouldn't have picked him for you. You go more for the cerebral type. What drew you guys to each other?"

"Crazy hot chemistry," a voice says over my shoulder, and then there is a big, strong body at my back. Tight against my back. Two strong arms wrapped around me. There's heat everywhere, and a sweet tickle of beard and soft hair before lips touch my neck.

I gasp.

It's not for effect. It's because the combined feel of Clark, big and hard behind me, and the tingling along every nerve ending on that side of my body has gone straight to where it counts. My body goes liquid and needy.

It feels so good—*I* feel so good—that it actually takes me a moment to register the shock on Reuben's face.

Ha.

Take that, asshole.

It takes me another moment to realize that I guess this means Clark and I aren't "breaking up" today.

10

CLARK

The eyes on us are even sharper tonight. When Jessa excuses herself to go to bed, everyone turns to look at me.

"I'll be there as soon as everyone else turns in, babe," I tell her. The term of endearment feels surprisingly good on my tongue. "I gotta stay with the fire till then."

I'm hoping if I stay in the clearing long enough, Reuben and Corinna will confine their extracurriculars to their tent, Jessa will fall asleep, and I won't do something I'll hate myself for afterwards.

I can still feel the imprint of her whole body against mine from when I intervened to save her from Reuben's prying. Lithe and soft and somehow—even frozen—full of life, as live as an electrified wire. All of that electricity pouring into me.

I managed to pull away just before I embarrassed both of us (again).

A glance flies back and forth between Amanda and Kane. I brace myself. Sure enough, Kane says, "You go ahead, lover boy. I'll stay with the fire."

I glare at him, but despite his boy-next-door sweetness, he's Wilder steel, and just smiles back.

So instead of guarding the fire, I'm standing by Jessa's side, and we're brushing our teeth in companionable silence. Spitting, filling in our leave-no-trace toothpaste pits, dropping our cosmetics together into the same bear bag, strolling back to the tent. She gets in first, and I follow. Like last night, we press to the opposite sides of the tent, as far away from each other as possible.

"I'll try not to—"

"You're fine," she says. "You can't help it that I'm so magnetic."

I laugh.

For a while after that, in the dark of the tent, we pretend we're going to go to sleep right away.

I can hear her breathing, though. It's not sleep breathing.

After a while, she says, "Clark?"

"Mmm-hmm?"

"You awake?"

"No." It's childish, but it makes her laugh anyway.

When she stops giggling, she says, "We're going to need an exit strategy."

"Huh?"

"Like, a way to get out of this without either of us having to admit it was an act."

"Oh. Right."

"It'll be easy once we're home. You can just tell your sibs that it didn't work out. You can say I was too uptight or cold or whatever for you. Or that I wasn't into hiking and camping enough."

"But none of those things is true."

She's not uptight or cold. And she's plenty into hiking and camping. She's kept up with me at every pass, and tonight she used the bow to start a fire and coax it to life, with no help.

I watched from a distance, the way she crouched over the small coals and patiently fed them. *I want someone to pay attention to me like that,* I thought, and told myself the ache I felt was the old familiar distress of missing Emma.

She makes a small noise, like a huff. "It's also not true that we're dating. So why does the breakup story have to be true?"

"I don't know. I just don't like the idea of using your ex-husband's bullshit excuse for being a cheating asshole."

"Excuse?" She tilts her head.

"Yes, excuse! He said that mean shit about you to make it okay that he did something completely vile!"

I turn my head to look at her. She's staring at the top of the tent, looking sad. I hate it. I want to roll over and put my arms around her.

"Don't buy his bullshit, Jessa. He sold you that crap to make it easier for him to leave. Because he was horny and selfish."

She turns her head and smiles at me. "You think?"

"I know it. And, by the way, 'slow to warm up' isn't a bad thing. I like people who are slow to warm up."

My mind serves me an image of how it would feel to warm Jessa up... with a kiss. With butterfly touches. Until she's moving under me like she did in last night's dream.

Oh. Wow.

I shut that mental movie down quickly.

"You're slow to warm up," she says, not knowing how wrong she is at the moment. "I never heard you say more than two words to me before last night."

She's still smiling at me. I smile back. It feels ridiculously good, but also challenging, like those muscles are stiff from long disuse.

She turns away again, and sighs. "But we still need a reason to break up."

That's not difficult. It's not even a lie. "I realized I'm still not ready for another relationship. It's too soon."

She shifts in the sleeping bag, a slide of nylon against skin that I can feel in my own body. "Is that true?"

"Yeah. I don't want to fall in love ever again."

"Have you—" She stops. "You know what? None of my business."

"Only super casual. One-night stuff." I answer the question she wouldn't let herself ask. I'm not sure why I do, except that speaking truth into the darkness of the tent is easy. Maybe it's the fact that we're not facing each other. The fact that the whole thing's a pretense. Maybe inside a lie, you can tell the truth without consequences.

She's quiet on the other side. So quiet I can hear her breathing, can hear the play of her fingers over the slippery exterior of her sleeping bag.

"I don't want to, either," she says. "Fall in love again. I see all these people get married, and they're so sure they're doing the right thing, but they're only right half the time. Less than half the time."

"You're a cynical wedding planner."

"Yeah. Since Reuben. I wish I weren't, but he broke something in me, and I haven't been able to enjoy a wedding since."

For some reason that makes me really sad.

"I think it's because it was so humiliating. I can remember

the humiliation so much more strongly than the feeling of being in love with Reuben. All those people who knew."

My chest opens up, serving me a sloppy portion of unwanted memory. "Like grief," I say. "I just wanted to be alone, and all those people wanted a part of me. Of her."

"I'm sorry," she says. "I think I was one of those people. With my casserole."

"Wait, what?" I'm confused.

"I dropped the casserole, and we bumped heads."

I shake my head. "I'm sorry. I don't remember much of that night."

"You don't need to apologize! You were grieving. But," she says, biting her lip. "If you feel like apologizing for something, you were a bit of a dick at the literacy fundraiser."

I recall it in my mind's eye, all the parts I pushed down to the bottom of my mind, now too clear for comfort. The swerve of her dress's neckline over the pretty pale globes of her tits. The curve of her lips, the sparkle in her eyes. The sense of wanting to know what was making her smile. That night was the first time since Emma's death that desire started in my chest and not my cock, like something inside me was reaching out to something inside her. I wanted it to go away. I wanted her to go away.

So I was a dick.

But right now? I don't want her to go away. I want her to come closer.

I want to taste the curve of that smile.

"You were pretty," I say. "I didn't want you to be pretty."

It's a fraction of the truth, but across the tent, she makes a small, startled noise.

I roll towards her at the same time she rolls towards me,

our mouths meeting in the dark. It's a sweet shock of wet heat, and my body responds, fast and furious, zero to sixty. I clutch her head and kiss her again, licking into her soft, responsive mouth, tasting the little sounds she makes. "Shh," I say, pulling back for a second. "Unless you want Reuben to know. In which case, yell it to the stars. Tell him how good it feels."

It does. So good, my whole body is on fire. I kiss her again, and her hand finds the back of my head, tugging me closer, her mouth taking sips and bites of mine. I shove the sleeping bag away, and down, wanting to get all these fucking layers out from between us.

"Clark!" a voice calls, startlingly close to my head. "We have an emergency out here."

11

JESSA

Clark leaps into action, rolling away from me, grabbing his boots, and sliding out of the tent at warp speed.

Kane's outside, and in a few words, he outlines the situation.

The emergency was caused by Reuben, who decided it would be a great idea to take a midnight hike with Corinna. They were apparently searching for some nearby waterfalls where you can skinny dip. Instead, Reuben tripped on the way back and sliced the hell out of his leg. He probably needs stitches. Kane thinks Clark might have to hike out with him on his back as soon as there's light in the sky.

"I only have one of the smaller first aid kits. We need the big emergency one."

"On it," Clark says, digging in his pack. "Shit. Some of the ointments and stuff are in the bear bag."

"I'll get them. You go deal with the injured dumbass. Maybe next time you need to be clearer about what constitutes stupid."

"I didn't think I had to explain that hiking by yourself in the dark, in the middle of the night, without a guide was stupid."

"Yeah, well. Stupid always finds a way to think it isn't."

"Where is he?"

"By the fire. One of us needs to get it going again, the other one needs to tend to him."

I stick my head out of the tent. The two Wilders, silhouetted against the moonlit sky, are huge over me. "Do you need my help?"

"No," Clark says. "Stay here. Sleep."

He gives me a look I can't read. Apology, I think.

They're gone.

I lie in the dark, wondering what the hell just happened and what to make of it. The intimacy of our conversation, how close to the heart we got.

I don't want to ever fall in love again.

He broke something in me, and I haven't been able to enjoy a wedding since.

I hadn't told anyone that before.

I wonder if he'd told anyone what he told me. I'm guessing not.

I let myself think about how he explained his behavior that night at the fundraiser.

You were pretty. I didn't want you to be pretty.

My whole body went hot at those words. Not just sex-hot, although that too. But warm all over.

And that kiss.

Holy shit, that kiss.

Soft mouth and rough beard and Clark's big hand pinning my head in place.

I would have let him do anything to me. Even though we'd just finished telling each other that we would never be with anyone else in a way that we'd let matter.

Maybe because we'd just finished telling each other that.

I guess we both felt like, with all that truth on the table, it might be safe to take what we needed.

I guess I should be grateful to Reuben for interrupting, because I have no idea what would have happened if he hadn't.

Apparently, the universe sent Reuben on this trip for a good reason.

I WAKE up when Clark crawls back in. He brings a blast of cool damp outside air, the smell of blood and fire, and then, as he settles down, a sudden wave of warmth I can feel from my side of the tent.

"You okay?" I ask him sleepily.

"I'm fine. Your jackass ex not so much, but we patched him up best we could and I'll hike out with him at dawn. I'm going to try to grab a couple of hours sleep between now and then."

"Makes sense."

He wraps himself in his sleeping bag, and I think that's it. His breathing evens out, and if I hadn't heard the exact cadence of his not-quite-snores last night, I'd think he was asleep—but I know he's not.

"And Jessa?"

"Yeah?"

"I'm sorry."

I hear my own breath huff into the quiet tent in the dark.

"About earlier," he clarifies, as if I could have thought he meant anything else. "I shouldn't have crossed that line. You're Emma's friend. That makes this impossible. And I didn't even ask—"

"You didn't do anything wrong," I say.

That makes this impossible, he said. For him? For me? For both of us? I want to ask—but I don't. What's clear here is that he's pushing me away. That he's sorry it happened.

And that's definitely for the best, because like he said, he's not ready for a relationship. And I'm leaving in September to live on the other side of the country.

"We both wanted that kiss."

He laughs, small and rough. "I guess we did. Still. I shouldn't have crossed the line."

"It's okay," I say. "We both crossed it. But we can, you know, uncross it."

He laughs.

I think I will never not love making Clark Wilder laugh. Especially now that I know a hundred percent for sure he doesn't hate me.

"Consider it uncrossed," he says.

And that's it.

I lie awake for a while until I hear Clark breathing buzzily—his not-quite-snoring. And then I drift back off, and when I wake up again, he's gone.

After one of Amanda's fabulous breakfasts, the Gilderness trip hikes out of the woods without Clark.

Kane and Amanda send us on our way with a few more bits of Wilder swag and a warm invitation to come on more Gilderness and survival trips, as well as Brody's Boat events.

I tuck the brochures into my bag, feeling oddly melancholy.

12

CLARK

Reuben survives his brush with stupidity, earning himself forty-seven stitches and an antibiotic shot. I get home, shower, unpack, and obey a summons from Gabe to get my ass to his house for a family dinner.

There are Wilders *everywhere* when I arrive. Our numbers keep increasing. I mean, technically not all the add-ons are officially Wilders, but I feel like it's only a matter of time. At the rate at which my brothers are pairing off, there will be no man left standing by next year.

I mean, besides me.

And probably Easton. Let's face it. He's not husband material. And he'd be the first to tell you that.

Amanda and Lucy are on the front porch, where Amanda's four-year-old son Kieran, still obsessed with the rocking chair, is catching air off some of his more violent rockings. Periodically Amanda tries unsuccessfully to rein it in, then shrugs and gives up.

I greet the women with hugs.

"How was the trip?" Lucy asks.

I try to read from her expression whether Amanda has already ratted me out. I suspect the answer is yes, but what I don't know is which version of reality she gave them. Am I dating Jessa? Or pretending to date Jessa?

Lucy's expression is neutral, and I deliberately don't look at Amanda. Even so, I can feel her smirking.

"Trip was good," I tell Lucy. "Until I had to hike out this morning with a guy on my back who decided it would be a good idea to go on an unguided midnight hike."

Lucy winces. "I guess part of the point of the Gilderness trips is to weed those ones out before they go on actual survival trips?"

"I wouldn't put it past this one to show up for another trip. Can we blackball dumbasses from future trips?"

Lucy shrugs. "I don't see why not. As a private trip leader, we reserve the right to refuse service to anyone for any reason. I'll start a dumbass spreadsheet."

Of course she will. Lucy's the best. Also disruptively beautiful: She almost started an inter-sibling war between Easton and Gabe when she came to town. She has long blond hair, usually worn in long ringlets, a sweetly pretty face, and big blue eyes. She'd be a fairytale princess if she weren't also such a hardass.

If she's heard that I'm dating—or "dating" Jessa—I don't see signs of it in the way she looks at me.

Whew. The whole thing feels like a grenade with the pin pulled out.

I haven't raised the subject of our dating or our "breakup" because I don't want to wake a sleeping beast. It's probably the kind of thing that will just die away without any effort on my part, since I'm pretty sure both Amanda and Kane knew it was a pretense. But if anyone asks, I can always claim Jessa and I broke up, as we'd agreed to.

I mean, in a manner of speaking, we did. We had a short, very sexy fling in the tent last night, consisting of the hottest kiss known to humankind, and then we declared the whole thing over.

Which doesn't stop me from reliving the kiss. Where did she learn to kiss like that? Why is her mouth so fucking soft? Why did her tongue feel so damn good against mine, in ways that made my body and mind go straight to other questions? Such as, What would that tongue feel like on the head of my cock? These, and many other inquiries, will go unanswered.

I head through the house. The kitchen is packed with Wilders and Wilder-adjacent friends. Antonio and Maria Perez—the parents of my brother Brody's girlfriend, Rachel —are cooking Cuban food, along with my mom, my mom's bunco friend Geneva, and Lucy's mom, Adele Booth. And— as of this weekend!—Lucy's stepdad, Gregg Booth. I greet everyone with hugs. No pointed questions from anyone in there, so I mark myself "safe" and head out back.

Kane and Gabe are tending the grill while Hanna, Kane's ski-biz partner—and Easton, my youngest brother and Wilder's resident god of casual sex—are playing a netless version of badminton in the backyard, arguing about the non-existent rules of the non-existent game. That's classic for the two of them. Easton and Hanna have been fighting nonstop since Gabe and Kane brought Hanna into the business. On the surface, their fight is about everything and nothing, but especially Easton's unrepentant plan to work his way through earth's entire female population and Hanna's equal- and-opposite lack of interest in dating.

I clap Gabe on the back, and he claps me back. Of all my brothers, he and I are the most alike, and have the easiest relationship. We get each other. If I actually said shit like this, I'd say he was my best friend.

"You're the last one to arrive," he tells me.

"Where are Brody, Rach, and Justin?" Justin is Brody's son—the adoption just went through.

"RVing cross-country. They decided to turn it into a yearly tradition. They'll be back later this week."

Then he calls over my head. "Hey—everyone. Grab everyone. Grab Lucy. We have an announcement to make."

My heart starts pounding, and I wish like hell, like I do whenever big stuff happens, that Emma were here. I still don't want anything big—good or bad—to happen without her. I still don't want life to go on in her absence.

But nothing galvanizes Wilders like news, and a moment later everyone is in the backyard.

Gabe puts his arm around Lucy, draws her close to his side, and drops the world's best bombshell:

"Lucy and I are engaged. And we're having a baby."

THERE'S SCREAMING and jumping and hugging and hooting. I might even be involved, at least in the hugging. I think I can, legit, claim not to have screamed or hooted. I think.

As you might imagine, it takes a while for the excitement to die down, but once it does, we get the scoop. It was the day of Lucy's mom's wedding. They were about to board the boat where the wedding was being held, and Lucy fessed up that she was pregnant. And Gabe popped the question.

"Shotgun wedding!"

"I already had the ring and the proposal queued up," Gabe says. "So even though I did propose after she told me she was pregnant, I don't think you can call it a shotgun wedding."

Lucy is beaming, and I have to admit that now that I know she's pregnant, I can see the glow.

Gabe puts his arm around her and squeezes her to his side. "That said, we're going to do it quick, because after that the weather will suck, and also because Lucy wants to wear Mom's wedding dress—"

"And I'll have a belly after September and won't be able to fit into Barb's dress." She smooths her hands over her still-flat midsection.

Gabe nods. "We're going to throw an official engagement party in two weeks at our place. You're all invited—and plus ones, too."

Hanna's head swivels toward me. "Are you going to bring your girlfriend?"

It takes me a second to realize a) she's talking to me, and b) everyone—family, friends—an entire backyard full of people—are staring at me, waiting for my answer.

Holy shit.

How does Hanna know I have a girlfriend?

Wait a second.

I don't have a girlfriend.

How does Hanna know I have a *fake* girlfriend? Did Amanda tell her?

I glare across the yard at Amanda. She shakes her head,

and mouths, *Not me!* And I can tell she's telling the truth. She looks as confused as I feel. Plus, she may be evil but she's not *that* evil.

I'm caught off guard and flustered, and I can't get my brain working. It's a big blob of:

What the fuck? And *What do I say?* And *How did this happen?*

"You have a girlfriend?"

That voice, the one filled with wonder and joy, belongs, of course, to my mother.

13

JESSA

"Wait. You want us to turn down the Darman-Stevens wedding *why*?"

Imani stands in the doorway of my office at The Best Day, forehead wrinkled in confusion.

Clearly she has just read my email. Also, clearly the question is rhetorical, because I told her in the email *why* I think we should turn down the wedding.

"It's a PR stunt, not a marriage," I reiterate. "It's performance art, not a wedding."

"You don't know that." She crosses her arms over her ridiculously adorable outfit. Imani is cute a hundred percent of the time, and today is no exception. She is wearing an orange jumpsuit with sunshine yellow flowers that looks absolutely perfect with her cool, dark brown skin and tight natural curls.

I raise my eyebrows at her. "Let's review. Two dating gurus, one who champions casual sex with no attachment and the other who is the most hopeless romantic on earth, are getting very, publicly married and live-streaming the event on both their YouTube channels. How could that possibly be anything other than a stunt?"

"I think it's the most romantic thing I've ever heard! It's like, the perfect rom-com!"

I roll my eyes. "It's total and complete bullshit."

"Jessa," Imani says sternly. "You cannot let your cynicism color your decision-making. We *have* to do this wedding."

I sigh.

"A, it's really my call."

I close my eyes. I know she's right. When I leave Rush Creek this fall for the East Coast, I'm selling the business to Imani. So even though I'm used to making the decisions up to this point, this isn't really my decision to make.

"Point taken," I say.

"B, you need the money."

I close my eyes.

"Don't do the guilt spiral!" she commands. "Don't do it! It's not your fault she turned out to be the scum of the earth!"

She's talking about our ex-employee, Bonnie, who I hand-picked while Imani was on a long sabbatical to tend to her ailing parents. After about six months of working for The Best Day, Bonnie stole two big weddings from us with a lie—that we had double-booked ourselves and were going to cancel on both of them. She also stole our client database and spread the word that we *had* double-booked ourselves and canceled late on our clients. She used the stolen intellectual property and our damaged reputation to leverage herself into a wedding business that directly competes with ours.

Imani and I leapt into action and repaired a lot of relationships, but it's hard to undo a smear campaign. You're always playing catch-up. It's been a few months since

Bonnie's pillage, and I still have clients bail out on me after they catch wind of the scandal.

Kyle Darman and Brandi Stevens, however, were totally unconcerned about the scandal. Kyle went to school with Imani and says he trusts her like his own sister. Which may partly explain why I'm getting no traction on turning down the job.

I open my eyes to find Imani watching me with a gentle expression. She fidgets with her necklace, her unconscious habit, then tilts her head and frowns at me. "No guilt spiral," she says sternly. "Everyone makes mistakes."

"You wouldn't have if you'd been here."

She's never going to convince me I didn't let us both down by trusting Bonnie.

"You have no way to know that," Imani says. "You have to stop beating yourself up about it. It's bad enough that you're punishing yourself by quitting the wedding business and moving to the ends of the earth."

"I'm not punishing myself!" I protest. "The East Coast is not the ends of the earth. Besides, I'm moving to be closer to Madison."

She just gives me The Eyebrows.

I cross my arms, and Imani does a little whole body shrug to show she's backing off. "Whatevs," she says. "But Jessa, hon, you're the one who said you don't want to have to use Reuben's book money for the business."

I used a lot of my personal funds to repair the damage that Bonnie did to the business. My savings account is depleted, and the business won't be able to pay me back without the Darman-Stevens wedding—which means it'll be hard to get my footing after a cross-country move. Unless I use Reuben's money. He owes me thousands more dollars as part of our divorce settlement. The payment was legitimately delayed because he was waiting for royalties on The Book—the one where I play the bitchy wife who deserved to be ditched. He has the money now, but so far, I've donated every check he's sent me to non-profits, because I don't want the business to grow on the seeds of my own humiliation.

"If we take the Darman-Stevens wedding, you can pay yourself back and you can keep donating Reuben's nasty-ass, dirty book-money to women's shelters."

She's making a strong point here, so I counter with: "Do you really think it's good for our—your—brand to be associated with the Darman-Stevens thing?"

"Hell, yes! Have you seen how many YouTube subscribers they have? That's not taking into account their Insta and TikTok followers. And I'm not even talking about all the other platforms."

"But we—you—don't need a national following. You need local reach."

"Weddings aren't a local business anymore, hon. Rush Creek is a destination."

Imani's right. I know she's right.

She knows she's right, too, and presses her advantage. "Kyle Darman and Brandi Stevens could be the real thing. Open your heart and mind." She makes a face at me, like she knows she's pushing her luck, but it does make me smile.

She knows how it is for me. I grew up flipping through my mom's novels to find the love scenes, and when I discovered romance novels, I was elated to find that there was a whole genre of books for people just like me, who thought romantic love made the world go 'round. I used to think weddings were the most romantic days on earth, that I had the best job anyone could possibly imagine.

It doesn't make Imani or me happy that Reuben killed that part of me.

"If you take lead on it, we can do it," I concede, and she beams at me.

I make a you-win-but-I-don't-like-it face at her. She shrugs, still grinning. I decide it's time for a new topic.

"How's Jada doing with the cast?"

Imani rolls her eyes. "I wish they'd made it any color but pink. Her new favorite game is, she's an injured princess and I have to wait on her."

I can't help my snicker.

"You come over and play lady-in-waiting!" Imani says, outraged, but she's laughing, too.

"Hello?" a deep voice calls from our office waiting area.

Wait a second. I *know* that voice.

Whhhhhaaattt the fuck? I mouth to Imani.

"Clark?" I call back.

"Hey," he says, appearing behind Imani. Towering over her, to be exact. Imani's not tiny, either. He's wearing jeans and a t-shirt that says: "It's Wilder in the Woods," with the Wilder Adventures logo underneath.

I can attest to that.

Imani turns and sees him, then rounds back to me with a big *wow* face. Since I'm facing him, I can't really respond, but I think she can probably tell from the fact that I've stopped breathing that something's up.

"Oh, hey," he says to Imani.

"Clark, this is my business partner, Imani Jones. Imani, this is Clark Wilder."

"Oh, you're one of them," she says.

The corners of his mouth twitch. "One of who, exactly?"

"Wilder brothers. We call you the Mountain Men of Rush Creek."

"And by 'we' she doesn't mean me," I assure him. "I haven't even heard that."

He leans against the wall and manages to look completely at home there, like he's holding up the wall instead of the other way around. He looks from Imani to me. "I have a question for Jessa."

"I'll leave you two to your discussion," Imani says, giving me one more open-mouthed *wa-wa-wow* before she darts around him to her office.

Clark steps into my office. It's teeny to begin with, but with a mountain man in it, it feels a whole lot smaller. Like that tent we shared. I can smell pine forest, soap, and shampoo. I should probably stop thinking about burying my face in his T-shirt and sucking his scent down like nectar.

My face gets hot.

That kiss. I've tried everything in my power to put it out of my head, but I've failed. I failed most notably last night in the privacy of my own bed, a hand between my legs and the vivid memory of Clark's mouth urging me on.

"So, um, what brings you here?" I manage. I also (somehow) manage not to fan myself with papers on my desk. He looks *so* good. He trimmed his beard since the end of the trip, and I want to touch it.

I want to feel it against my face.

I want to feel it a few other places, too.

"I have a favor to ask you."

"Shoot," I say. My heart is pounding. What kind of favor

could we possibly be talking about? The good kind? The kind I'd really like to grant?

The kind that would make a slightly awkward and messy situation *even* more awkward and messy?

Clark winces. "This is kind of—I'm sorry about this." If his eyebrows get any lower, they're going to prickle his eyeballs.

I get the feeling that Clark Wilder apologizes infrequently and only in extreme situations—so that worries me a bit.

"If this puts you in a difficult situation, I understand. Don't say yes unless you feel like you're comfortable with it."

"You're scaring me," I tell him bluntly.

That makes him smile, which makes it all worse. Straight white teeth, a curve to his soft lips, and crinkles at the corners of his beautiful gray eyes. "Well. It's a little scary. I won't lie." He's still smiling. "It turns out that Kane bought that we were dating. He bought it so hard that he told his business partner, Hanna, that we were. And Hanna, who isn't known for discretion under the best of circumstances, asked me, in front of my entire family—including my mom—if I was bringing my 'girlfriend' to my brother's engagement party, which is happening next weekend. Not this coming one, the next one."

I stare at him, open-mouthed.

He ducks his head, sheepish.

"You didn't tell them we broke up." It's not really a question.

"My mind honestly went blank."

"You could still tell them we broke up?" That's definitely a question.

"I *could*. But—" He closes his eyes, screws up his face. I

think he's pleading with me. "—my mom was so fucking happy."

"Clark," I say sternly. Someone around here has to face the facts. "We can't fake date forever. Eventually we'll have to 'break up.' And won't she be even more unhappy then?"

"No, I really don't think so. I think she's been praying for evidence that I'm not permanently broken. I think this will get her off my back. If she sees that I can move on then I think she'll stop feeling like it's her job somehow to fix me."

I squint at him.

"Please, Jessa," he says.

There is a Wilder in my office. He is the most beautiful man I know. He kisses like a dream. And he is begging me to go to a party with him.

Fake-go to a party with him.

But *still*.

I am not strong enough to withstand this.

"Okay?" I attempt.

"Are you asking me or telling me?"

"Both?"

That makes Clark laugh out loud, and the last drops of resistance drain from my soul. "Okay," I say, more firmly.

"Thank you. Thank you, thank you." His eyes are soft. Warm.

Ah. Gratitude really is hot. Even the non-sexual kind. My office suddenly feels like it's a thousand degrees. "You're, um, welcome."

"We should plan a time to get our ducks in a row. Sort out our stories, get on the same page."

"Aren't we a little late with that?"

He frowns. "Just because you survived Amanda and Kane

doesn't mean you're ready for my mom and Gabe. And that's not even taking into account Rachel, Lucy, Hanna, Brody, and the grandmas."

"I'm feeling scared again."

He crosses his arms and looks fierce, which does problematic things to my panty region. "Don't worry. I've got you."

Terrifyingly, I'm afraid he does.

"Give me your phone. I'll put in my number. You can let me know when you're free for getting on the same page."

Somehow, despite being the owner of my own company and not the kind of person who takes orders from anyone who isn't wearing white or footing the bill, I hand my phone over. It is tiny in his big paw. I have immediate, vivid fantasies of other places I would like him to put that hand.

When he's gone—his number in my contacts and a text sent to his phone—Imani comes back into my office, fanning herself. "What was *that*?" she asks.

I bite my lip. "You have time for a long story?"

"Always." She plops herself down in one of my guest chairs.

Starting with her own cancellation phone call to me, I tell her the whole tale of the Gilderness trip. When I get to the part where Clark says, "She's with me," she slides all the way off the chair and onto the floor.

"Yeah," I agree.

She hoists herself back up and I reel out the rest of the story, right up to the kiss.

"Holy crapton of hotness! So now you're—a couple?"

I shake my head. "No. Now we're a fake couple."

I tell her how we agreed not to mess around—because of

Emma, or at least that was what he said. Then I explain why he showed up in our offices today.

She wrinkles her nose, her eyebrows drawing together. "Do you think..."

"Do I think what?"

"Do you think it's a ploy to get more time with you?"

I shake my head. "No. I think he's for real. I think his wife's death destroyed him and he needs to get his family off his back."

She puts a finger to her mouth, then tilts her head. After a moment she squints at me. "I think he likes you."

I shake my head harder. "If he did, why wouldn't he just ask me out?"

"Because he's not ready to admit to himself that he likes you?"

I roll my eyes. "We're not in seventh grade."

Imani stares at me for a lifetime and a half, and I'm wishing she didn't know me quite so well. She tugs a curl, purses her lips, and eyes me some more, until I have to look away.

"The thing is, Jessa," she says, "we're all basically *always* in seventh grade when it comes to dating."

14

CLARK

I step out of the offices of The Best Day feeling strangely cheerful.

Seeing Jessa put me in a better place. She makes me laugh.

And she was willing to help me out. That felt good.

Also, I like looking at her. Today, her straight hair was pulled back in a ponytail. She was dressed for work, in a pair of black pants and a loose, silky-looking top the color of red wine. Her shoulders were bare and satiny looking, and the top dipped so I could see the shadow of her cleavage. She wore high heels that matched her shirt, and I tried not to think about those heels and how they would make her almost my height, so that if I pushed her flush against a wall and kissed her, we would fit together perfectly.

I'm not going to kiss her again.

That's not the point of having her be my date at the engagement party.

Although it occurs to me that a kiss or two, just for plausibility, might make sense.

My cock gets heavy at the thought.

I yank my mind back to the present and head to street level via a flight of exterior steps. Jessa's office is over Krandall's Outdoor Store, right in the heart of Rush Creek.

The town is so different now from the one I grew up in. Lots of stores are still here, including Krandall's, as well as the tack shop and the feed store, but those stores stock completely different items now. Like Krandall's sells bikini bathing suits and coverups and wedding favors, and the feed store has cut back its hours and filled a number of its shelves with grocery items.

I'm headed there right now, actually, because Gabe asked me to pick up a bag of food for his bottomless pit of a dog, Buck. I'm crossing the feed store parking lot, headed for its front door, when I nearly crash into someone.

"Clark," a woman says.

Recognizing her voice, I pull back. "Jeannie."

I don't mean my tone to sound as dull as it does. It just plummets like that, flatlines. Because the woman standing in front of me is someone I usually try to avoid as much as possible: Emma's mom, Jeannie. Normally I'd cross streets and duck into stores to avoid running into her, but I can't do that now. We're face-to-face.

My chest feels like it's stuck in a hydraulic press.

"How've you been?"

Jeannie's smiling at me, for the first time I can remember since Emma passed. Pink-cheeked and less drawn, she looks a lot better than the last time I saw her. Like Emma, Jeannie's petite and raven-haired, though Jeannie's hair is streaked with gray.

Meeting her today is fucked up timing in light of the fact

that I just invited a woman to pretend to be my serious girlfriend.

"Not too bad," I manage.

"Yeah?" she says. "You look good."

"Thanks. You too."

She tilts her head. "What are you up to?"

Lying about my romantic life to get family members off my back, sharing a tent with a woman I have no business lusting after, and generally making a hash out of things. "Uh, this and that. We've been trying to expand Wilder Adventures by marketing to spa-goers and bridal parties and all that." I doubt Jeannie gives a crap about my business model, but it's the best I can do. "To fit with where Rush Creek is going overall."

Fortunately, she musters some interest. "Yeah? And how's that going?"

"I mean, not too bad. We're making progress. Business is up a bit. It's a lot of work. Like I just bought these Airstreams I have to renovate, and now I need to hire a designer. But it's good. We're getting there. And what are you up to?"

As soon as the words are out of my mouth, I regret them. Last time I'd asked her that, it was clear she was barely getting out of bed in the morning. My guilt had closed in on me. I'd barely staggered away from her before gulping air in the privacy of my car; it was the next closest thing to a panic attack.

But now she smiles again. "I've been working with a consumer advocacy organization," she says. "They fight to get better warning labels on medications—and in extreme cases, to get them taken off the market. Usually it's through class action, but sometimes, like in this case, it's through letter writing campaigns. Actually, if you're interested, I'd love to have you write something—"

She looks me in the eye and something in my chest clamps down.

I don't want to have this conversation with her. The conversation about who's responsible for what happened to Emma. The conversation about what killed Emma.

I know my answer, and the answer is me.

"I—uh. I'll think about it." It comes out choked, barely audible, barely words.

She straightens up. "It's helped me, Clark. It's helped me to do something to make sure this doesn't happen to other people's daughters and wives—"

"Uh, yeah. I'll think about it for sure."

It wouldn't have happened to Emma if I'd listened to her. If I'd taken her seriously. But I didn't.

I had one job, to protect my wife, and I didn't do it.

She puts out a hand, touches my bare forearm. "Clark."

Her hand is small and cool, like Emma's was.

I finally draw a breath that's deep enough.

"No pressure, hon," she says. "It's just a possibility. Keep it in mind." Her green eyes are quiet and gentle on my face.

"I will."

She touches my arm again. "Take care, hon. And don't be a stranger. I miss you."

"Miss you, too," I say.

But as she walks away and I struggle to even out my breathing, I know I'll be a stranger to her for a while longer, if not forever.

I'm still a stranger to myself.

15

JESSA

After a series of back-and-forth text messages, Clark and I decide that we should meet at my apartment to work out our cover story. If we meet anywhere in town, it will be too easy for bystanders to overhear, and then it might get back to Clark's family—or Reuben.

Right before Clark is supposed to come over on Tuesday evening, he texts:

Okay if I bring takeout pizza for us?

I text back a thumbs up. And do a little happy dance. Because any guy who brings food when he comes to my house gets bigtime bonus points.

He gets *bonus* bonus points for asking first, in case I already had planned the menu—which I had, but since my plan was to eat packaged mac and cheese, I decided I could probably live with abandoning it.

Toppings?

I eat everything.

Meat lovers okay?

Perfect.

He knocks on the door. I open it to find him leaning against the far wall, pizza and a six pack of beer in hand. He's wearing jeans again, but this time with an Oxford button-down rolled to the elbows. Gah, those forearms really do it for me. Also, I wonder if he dressed to impress. If so, it's working.

Not that I liked the hiking pants and base layer shirt any less.

Actually, there's nothing Clark could do to hide the essential hotness of his big, hard body.

"Hey!"

"Hey, yourself."

"Come on in."

He does, filling my doorframe and then my sort-of-foyer.

"Cute place!" he says, looking around, and for unknown reasons, I blush.

"Thanks."

We're in the living-room-kitchen area, so he can see my hot pink couch, fluffy faux fur rug, and shelves and shelves of romance novels (which also tend toward the hot pink). I'm not ashamed of either my taste in books or my decor, but I did invite one date back here (fourth date), who was snarky about it.

I didn't sleep with him. Or go on a fifth date. Because who needs that kind of BS?

Clark surveys the room and says, "Now *that's* a couch."

I close one eye and assess him. "Are you mocking my couch?"

"Nope. I love that you have a hot pink couch."

I bite back a smile and think—for the first time—*Clark and I are friends.*

It's a really weird thought. I mean, I thought this guy hated me. And then we fake dated in a tent. And there was intense chemistry. And now we are fake dating some more.

Friends seems like a whole other thing.

But yeah.

I almost offer him a tour. But I stop myself just in time. The only rooms he can't see from where he is are my bedroom and bathroom. No need to go there. I already feel like he fills up the main room of my apartment with his mountain man self. Imagine how he'd be in my bedroom. It would be just him and my bed. No oxygen.

Instead, I lead him to the kitchen table, where he sets down the pizza and beer. "I didn't know if you drank. Or liked beer."

"I drink. And hate beer. But I have a bottle of wine open."

I grab the wine, a glass, and plates and napkins. "You want a glass?"

He shakes his head, cracks open a beer, and does that super-hot thing where he catches the foam with his open mouth, then licks his upper lip. There's a tiny bit of foam left there, and I lick my own lips reflexively.

We sit across from each other—Clark's legs taking up most of the space under my small table. I can feel the heat pouring off him. I wonder if I set the temp in my apartment too high. It's definitely warm in here. I gulp my wine.

"So, yeah. Getting our story straight," I say.

"You read all those books—?" He gestures at my bright-colored shelves. "You must have a good idea for how it was when we fake met. And where we went on our first fake date."

I hold back a smile. "I may have given it some thought."

He picks up his pizza, folds it in half, and swallows half the slice in a bite.

Wow. He is a big human. Pizza is disappearing into him at an alarming rate. I'm torn between wanting to grab slices and hoard them for myself, and being turned on by the sheer manliness of the display.

I force my mind back to our backstory. "We know we met in the first place because I was in Emma's book club, but we ran into each other on some kind of Mount Bachelor hike. That's what you told Reuben."

"Right."

"I'm thinking maybe I sprained an ankle and you had to give me a piggyback ride."

"Damsel in distress," Clark muses. "Don't you want a more badass role here? What if I sprained my ankle and you gave me a piggyback ride?" The corner of his mouth turns up, not quite a smirk.

"As much as I want to be badass, no one will believe that story."

Plus, I kind of like the version where Clark's hard torso is clutched in my thighs. I don't say that out loud, but I do feel the heat kick up into my cheeks. And glide down my belly to sink, liquid, between my legs.

Clark has very long eyelashes. And his eyes aren't just gray. They have flecks of other colors in them: green, brown, blue. He catches me staring and I glance away.

He makes a hmm noise. "Well, what if you rescue me some other way. What if I screw up my packing, and you have to rescue me by lending me a fleece jacket or something."

"And then when you gave it back to me, I liked the way it smelled so much I asked you out?"

He hoots out a laugh.

"You *think* I'm kidding."

It's Clark's turn to go slightly pink. "You like the way I smell." Not a question.

The air in the kitchen goes thick and still.

"Yeah. I do."

The moment is pregnant with possibility. He sets his slice down and stares at me. At my mouth. My breath speeds up.

And then he shrugs, sighs, raises his gaze to mine, and says, "That'll work as well as anything else."

Right. He's assuming I was faking it for the story. And I should be grateful for that, because otherwise, what was I thinking?

He finishes the slices he's working on, wipes his mouth on a paper napkin, and takes a long drink of beer. I watch his throat move and feel a tiny bit faint with lust.

"Where do we go on our first date?" he asks.

"Where would you take me?"

"Mmm," he says. "Dunno. It's—been a while since I've dated."

That shuts us both up for a minute.

He frowns. "Sorry. That was a downer, huh?"

"Don't worry about it," I tell him, meaning it. "I mean, you don't have to pretend with me. I knew her. I saw you two together. I *get* it. Be sad if you're sad."

His eyes flick to mine again, soft and grateful. The moment slows and freezes and I can't look away.

He does, first.

"Oscar's?" he hazards. Then he frowns. "I need to do better than that, huh?"

"I mean, I don't know? I love Oscar's. But is that your A-game date location?"

"Was it an A-game date?"

"Oh, *ouch*."

He winces. "Sorry. I didn't mean it like that. You're totally worth bringing the A game. I just meant, if we're going to break up after the party—we are going to break up after the party, right?"

"Uh—yeah?" I'm still stuck on, *you're totally worth bringing the A game*. What does he mean by that?

He breaks off another slice and tucks in. "If we're going to break up and it was never really, you know, *meant to be*, then I wouldn't have brought the A game to the first date. Or maybe we broke up because you sensed I never brought the A game."

I start laughing because he's so overthinking it. "What if I insist on choosing the location because I asked you out? And I take you for Korean barbecue?"

He raises his eyebrows. "I've never had Korean barbecue."

"All the more reason. You'd like it. They bring out a big platter or rack of meat, and the grill is set right into the table. It's all different kinds of meat—pork belly, bulgogi, galbi. We'd have that and loads of soju—you know what soju is?"

He shakes his head.

"It's this liquor made from starch, basically like vodka, except it's more like wine when it comes to alcohol content. Like fifteen percent. And it goes down super easy. You and I start talking and we're there for hours, drinking soju and barbecuing. There's a brand-new place in June River that doesn't have a limit on how long you can sit on weeknights. So we go on a Thursday night, and it's great. We have a blast."

He's watching me carefully, his pizza in suspended animation in his raised hand. "That sounds pretty fucking great."

"Well," I say, shrugging. "You can round up your brothers and we can all go sometime, after we decide we're better off as friends."

Is it my imagination, or does he look a little disappointed when I say that?

Do I feel a little disappointed?

"Do I ask you back to my place for a drink?" Clark asks.

"You do," I tell him. "But I say no. Because it's a first date."

His mouth tips up. "But I do try to kiss you. And you let me."

His voice is low and rough. My wine goes down the wrong pipe, and I have a coughing fit. When I recover, he changes the subject. "Obviously you haven't met my family. I guess I've been kind of taking things slowly because I'm still grieving."

"Right."

"Have I met yours?" He cocks his head, like something's just occurred to him. "Are they okay with your divorce and you dating again?"

I nod. "They never loved Reuben, it turns out, so they've been super supportive—although my mom has reminded me a few times that it's a good thing she's not my grandmother. She says we're probably all lucky her mom wasn't around for Madison's coming out or my divorce, or none of us would have heard the end of it." I shrug. "I guess it's possible they might think I should have given myself more time before dating again, but probably they'd just be psyched I'd found someone I liked."

"They sound pretty cool."

"Yup." I help myself to more pizza. "And yes, to bring this back to getting our stories straight, you totally would have met them."

I tell him they were here for a week, ending last weekend. "My mom bought out the Portland H Mart and descended with food and snacks for an army. When they found out I was dating someone who had already tried and loved Korean barbecue, my mom insisted that she and I cook you dinner. I tried to talk her out of it, but you assured me it wasn't a big deal, so that's what happened."

Clark looks a little green at the thought of this imaginary meet-the-parents.

"You were a good sport about it, though," I can't help throwing in. I'm enjoying myself way too much. My mom loves to feed people, and I imagine the idea of feeding someone as big and enthusiastic about his food as Clark would probably send her to the moon with joy.

"My mom made us doenjang jjigae—that's stew—and bibim negmyun—it's a kind of noodles—and seafood pancakes. Plus a ton of sides, including kimchi, of course. You loved everything, especially the spicy stuff. She kept offering you more food, and you kept accepting, until you realized that she wasn't going to stop until everything was gone. Also, she was super worried you didn't know how to make rice. She made you tell her your method, and then she told you how you were doing it wrong."

"Which I was," Clark says, getting into it. "I totally realized the error of my ways."

"And you guys loved each other."

Because I honestly think they would. My mom would get a kick out of Clark. My dad, too.

Clark stares at me steadily, holding my gaze with his gray eyes. "Of course I'd love them," he says. "Your parents. If they're anything like you."

Gobsmacked, I stare back at him, warmth creeping all over me, lighting up my nerve endings and tingling my nipples.

And then I remember:

He's faking it.

"Oh, damn!" I say. "You're, um, good at this."

He smiles at me. "We make a good team."

And despite the fact that I know all of this is just a story we invented, something in my chest blooms.

16

CLARK

The afternoon of Gabe's engagement party, I pick up Jessa at her place. When she answers the door, she's wearing a pretty, pale pink sundress.

"You look—really—that's." I nod toward her dress. "Well done on the costume choice," I say. "Good work. But you'll be cold." *And we'll be able to tell.* I try not to stare at the way the pale cloth hints at a low-cut lace bra underneath, her nipples two faint peaks. *Eye contact eye contact eye contact.*

Not gonna lie, sometimes being a decent guy is challenging. Jessa in that dress is one of those times.

Maybe she senses my difficulty, because she crosses her arms over her chest. *Thank you. That was helpful. Whew.* "It's warm now."

"It'll cool off. And we'll be outside a lot."

"I'll bring a coverup."

"Your legs will be cold."

My gaze falls to them, a lost battle. Long, perfectly shaped, smooth.

When I raise my eyes, she's smiling at me. *Busted.*

"I'll be okay," she says. "Let me just run back in and get a sweater for later."

When she comes back, I escort her to my pickup. I open the door on her side and offer her a hand up. She looks at it like it's slightly confusing, and for a second, I think she's going to refuse it. Her eyebrows draw together. "You don't have to pretend yet."

"I'm not pretending. I'm having manners."

Her eyebrows draw together. "It's the twenty-first century. Touching strange women isn't manners, it's creepy."

"You're not that strange," I say, with a shrug.

She presses her lips together against what I'm pretty sure is a laugh. Then she takes my hand, fingers strong and warm against mine. The skin-on-skin touch feels electric, and I have to stop myself from jerking away.

Just get through today.

That's been my refrain since we met to "get our stories straight." *Just get through the engagement party.* Then we can "break up" and get out of each others' hair before...

Before I tear the dress with my teeth.

I slide the key into the ignition and the truck's big engine roars to life.

"Can I get a Wilder family crash course on the way over?" she asks.

"Sure." I ponder where to start. "Gabe's—he's the oldest—and the one who's engaged. He's in charge. Of everything. Or he thinks he is, anyway."

"And he's marrying Lucy? The one who does the killer Wilder Adventures marketing."

"Exactly. She came to town from the East Coast, went

head-to-head with Gabe over how the business should be run, and, well, *won*."

She snickers. "That must have been something."

"Oh, it was." I smile, remembering the two of them striking sparks off each other. "The rest of us barely survived it."

I turn down the winding road to Gabe's place and the barn that houses the Wilder offices are located. "Brody's barely a year younger than Gabe. He's always felt like he was in Gabe's shadow. Took it out by being the bad boy of our crew. Until Rachel came home. She's Brody's best friend—Connor's—little sister, and kind of Brody's opposite. A librarian—or she was, anyway. She ended up helping him with these girls' nights on his boat—"

Jessa makes a small sound. She must know about Rachel's sex toy business.

"Yup," I say. "Those kinds of girls' nights."

"Oh, wow. Wish I'd been there for that."

"They could have sold front row seats. Anyway, then comes Kane." I hesitate. "I don't know what to say about Kane. He's just—Kane. He's the boy next door, as steady as they come. But..." I sigh. "I guess I don't know if he's really *happy*. The rest of us, we're Wilder Adventurers, through and through. But I guess somehow I think, with Kane, he's doing it because he feels like he has to, not because he loves it."

"I mean you'd have to figure that if there are five of you, one of you isn't going to be madly in love with the family business, right?"

"Right," I agree. "Just statistically speaking."

"And Amanda?"

He nods. "Amanda's had a tough couple of years. Three

little kids. Trying to get her catering business started. I don't think things were so great with Heath—her husband—for a while, either. But then after we did the Tinsel and Tatas Games and Gala last Christmas, something happened. She's been much happier since.

"And then Easton..." I pause. "We call him Easton the panty-melter. Not sure I need to say much more than that. He's the baby of the family, and, well, I don't think he's ever really felt the need to grow up."

"Makes sense." She tilts her head and rubs a palm across the dash of my truck. "But you left someone out."

"Who?"

"You, goofball."

That makes me smile. I shrug. "You know me. Grumpy but dependable."

"Oh, is that your tagline? I would have said 'One with the woods, a forest warrior, quick-thinking, great in an emergency, always willing to ride to a damsel in distress's aid, loyal family guy, steady as they come.'"

She catches me off guard, the praise too much and just right. I want to make her say it again, and I want to cover my eyes like a bashful kid.

"I like your version better," I say quietly. I cast a quick look her direction; she's looking back at me with something soft in her eyes that sets up an ache in my chest.

We pull up to the small lot in front of Gabe's house. She hops down before I can come around to open the door for her. We head up to the front of the house together, where we're greeted by a pack of wild children—Amanda's three and Brody's adorable toddler son, Justin.

"Uncle Clark!"

I'm swamped in hugs.

"Anna. Noah. Kieran. Justin," I count off, pointing for Jessa's benefit. "Kids, this is my friend Jessa."

"Mom says it's your *girlfriend* Jessa." Noah's almost eight and knows everything.

Jessa chuckles. "Yup. I'm his girlfriend Jessa."

I feel a small surge of satisfaction, just like I would if we were really dating and she'd owned it like that in front of the kids. Funny how easy it is to put on this act. Makes sense, I guess. They say even if you can't smile, fake smiling still releases all the same hormones.

Fake dating must be the same.

My mom is the next one out of the house, tailed by her friend Geneva. They're two founding members of the Bunco brigade, middle-aged white women with salt-and-pepper hair, though my mom's is bobbed and Geneva's is long and twisted up in a clip on her head. They've been friends for as long as I can remember.

"Clark!" my mom says, beaming. She wraps me up in a mom-scented hug, and even though her head doesn't reach my shoulder, I still get that burst of mom warmth and safety. She steps back and eyes Jessa with blatant curiosity. "And you must be Jessa."

"This is his *girlfriend* Jessa," Noah clarifies.

Jessa smiles at my mom. "Hi, Mrs. Wilder."

"Call me Barb," my mom says. "This is my friend Geneva."

I look at Noah. He looks back at me, a question on his face. I give him a teeny, tiny shrug.

But, huh. He could be onto something.

Geneva has been at my mom's side every time I've seen her for the past few months. Like, everywhere.

I wonder.

"Hi, Geneva," Jessa says. "Very nice to meet you both."

"We're so delighted to meet you, Jessa," my mom says, her smile growing even more outsized.

Mom, I inwardly groan. *Tone it down.*

As if I were worried about her scaring Jessa off. When the truth is that the reason Jessa's here is that she knows my mom is on my back.

"So you two met on a hiking trip?" Geneva asks.

"We did!" Jessa says. "Clark forgot to pack a fleece, so I lent him mine. And when he gave it back to me—"

We exchange panicked looks. The story sounded great in the privacy of her apartment, but faced with the reality of telling my mom that Jessa asked me out because she liked the way I smelled, we both balk.

My mom is looking from one of us to the other, her forehead wrinkled. Shit. She knows we're full of it. She knows the story is made up. She knows we're flailing and panicking. We're totally busted.

I open my mouth to jump in with the abandoned ankle-sprain story, in the hopes of salvaging the moment, but just then my mom's expression smooths into a huge smile. "Awwww!" she says. "Did it smell like him?"

Jessa blushes. "It did. And I won't say that's the only reason, but it definitely entered into why I asked him if he wanted to get dinner when we got back to civilization."

She pulls it off perfectly. If I didn't know better, I'd swear that's how it happened.

"That's exactly how Zach—Clark's dad—and I first got together. It was a kayaking trip and he lent me his wool sweater one night by the campfire. And then I basically refused to give it back." It's my mom's turn to blush. "Told him if he wanted it back he would have to take it."

"Mom!" I chastise.

Jessa turns to me. "I mean, you guys got here somehow, right?" She smiles at my mom. "I love that. Women who know what they want, for the win."

They beam at each other. I feel a surge of victorious pleasure. They like each other!

Wait.

Wait.

Wait.

It doesn't actually *matter* if they like each other.

Right?

Because...

This is an act.

"There's tons of food and drink in the kitchen," my mom says. "Go grab some."

As she ushers us forward, she mouths, "I like her" to me.

I try not to care.

We head into the kitchen, greeting people as we go. Amanda raises one eyebrow in my direction but says nothing, only introduces Jessa to her husband Heath.

Hanna and Easton are arguing over how much wine to put in the sangria, so I bypass them.

"This is my brother, Brody, and his girlfriend Rachel. Guys, this is Jessa."

Brody extends a hand and greets Jessa, squinting suspiciously at me as he does so. I give him an innocent shrug. After Amanda, if anyone is going to suss us out, it would be Brody.

"We've met," Rachel says, giving Jessa a hug. "I applaud your taste in women."

I look between them, but they both just smile. "What happens at the parties stays at the parties," Rachel says, shrugging.

Well, that's interesting. Rachel is working towards her degree and licensing to become a sex therapist. She also sells sex toys—I think technically she calls them intimacy aids—at parties that have become famous among folks in Rush Creek and with tourists. I wonder what Jessa did to earn her respect.

Women who know what they want, for the win, Jessa said.

She knew what she wanted when we were kissing. I can still hear those small, hungry sounds, feel the nip of her lips and the silk of her tongue. Her hands grabbing handfuls of my sweater.

How would it have been if we'd kept going? Like that, but a thousand times hotter?

Curiosity killed the cat, Clark Wilder.

"Can I grab you guys a drink?" Rachel asks.

"I'll take some of that sangria. If they've figured out the formula," Jessa says, tilting her head to consider Hanna and Easton.

"Anything hoppy for me," I say.

Rachel digs a beer from a cooler on the floor, hands it to me, and pours sangria for Jessa.

"Don't blame me if it sucks," Hanna says. Built like a woman rugby player, she has pale skin that sets off dark hair trimmed in an adorable pixie cut. I bet no one has ever applied the word adorable to her hair and lived to tell the tale, though. "Easton decided it needed more wine. There's not even anyone here for him to get drunk and take advantage of. Or at least not anyone he hasn't already slept with."

"I haven't slept with you," Easton points out.

"And you never, ever will," Hanna says fervently. "Something has to be off limits for Rush Creek's captain of puss—"

"This is Hanna," I jump in, before she can finish the word. "And my brother Easton. Oil—" I point to Hanna—"and water." I point to my brother.

He frowns. "That's not fair. It's more like she's broccoli and I'm chocolate ice cream."

"Or you're milk and I'm Red Bull."

We all wince.

"Right. Don't mix them. Got it."

Jessa greets them both, shaking hands with Easton and then hesitating before doing the same with Hanna. I watch Hanna's face as she logs Jessa's decision with approval.

In fact, everyone is beaming at us with that same absurd, doting smile that my mother wore earlier.

They're all unsettlingly happy for me.

Which of course makes me feel guilty. Both for the lie and because of... well, Emma.

They think I'm moving on.

I'm not moving on, I tell Emma in my head. *I'm doing this because I'm not ready to move on from you.*

And I can't feel guilty about that because Jessa knows exactly what I'm doing. She's doing it, too.

We're buying each other time and space.

17

JESSA

After we eat, I stand on Gabe's deck, watching Clark and Brody supervise a very loose game of almost-wiffleball among the kids. It's been going on a while now, but Justin just toddled up and begged to join, and after an exchange of baffled looks between Clark and Brody, they've let him in.

Clark kneels behind Justin, wraps his arms around Brody's son, and shows him how to swing the wiffleball bat. Clark's big hands cover Justin's tiny toddler hands, and they clobber the ball together. Justin watches wide-eyed as it sails off into the distance.

I get lightheaded from the ovary punch of that visual.

"Now we run," Clark says. He swoops up Justin and runs him to first, startling a belly laugh out of him.

I think I just dropped three eggs. It's a good thing Clark and I are faking it, because we'd totally be pregnant with triplets by midnight if we weren't.

"Not fair!" Kieran yells.

Clark grins at him. "You're bigger than he is!"

"But you're a lot bigger than I am!"

Smart kid.

"You want me to run you the next time it's your turn?" Clark asks.

"Yeah!" Kieran said.

"Okay. To be fair, I'll run anyone under five who wants to be run," Clark announces to the assembled kid pool.

"Who's going to run me?" Brody demands.

Clark deposits Justin on the makeshift first base and runs for Brody, jamming his shoulder into Brody's midsection and lifting him off the ground in a fireman's carry.

I can't hear the words Brody is hissing into his brother's ear, but I can guess at the gist. I'm hoping the kids can't hear, either.

"Pretty stinkin' cute, huh?" Rachel asks, coming up beside me. She's second generation Cuban-American, which accounts for her soft ponytail puff of dark brown hair and warm medium-brown skin. I found out her family heritage when I asked about the origin of the insanely delicious Cubano sandwiches we ate for lunch. The answer: Rachel's mom, Maria.

"They're adorable," I tell her.

She turns and gives me a knowing look. "And the little kids, too, right?"

I have a flash of confusion, caught between real and pretend, but then I remember that either way, the answer's the same. I smile back at her, like we're really both women lucky enough to have snared the attention of two of the hottest guys alive.

"Hey! Sorry I'm just getting a moment now to really say hi."

It's Lucy, her hair falling in too-pretty-to-be-real shiny blond ringlets, with makeup that looks like it was professionally done. If it weren't for the fact that Rachel, Hanna, and Amanda all look like ordinary people who rolled out of bed, checked a mirror for disasters, and showed up, I'd be feeling super intimidated right now.

(I don't want to admit how much effort I put into my own appearance. I told myself it was because I had to look like I was trying really hard to impress Clark's family... but I recognized it for the lie it was.)

"I'm so glad you could come!" Lucy says.

All of Clark's family has been super welcoming, to the point of being a tiny bit over the top. But I get it, I really do. They love him, and they've been worried about him. I feel simultaneously guilty about the deception and glad I could do something to soften the intensity of their attention on him.

"So you and Clark have been together... how long?"

"Just about a month."

"And you guys met on a hike?"

"Mmm-hmm," I say. Earlier, I thought we'd blown it with Clark's mom, and I'm a little wary of the fleece story now. But there's nothing for it: I say, "Believe it or not, he forgot to pack a fleece jacket, and I lent him one of mine."

"Clark did?"

"Right? I know. Mr. Prepared."

"I guess we all bork it sometimes. Nice to get to rescue the rescuer, huh?" She grins at me.

I grin back.

Just two women, lucky enough to be sleeping with two of the hottest—and most competent—guys in Rush Creek.

The moment of companionship feels waaay too good, and I have to remind myself: This is not actually yours.

The baseball game seems to have reached its natural end; Clark heads back onto the deck. He comes up behind me and loops his arms around me. "Hey, hon."

He feels good, warm and muscular. My body blooms and unfurls like it's too dumb to know the difference between fact and fiction. And let's face it: It is.

He ducks his head and drops a kiss near my ear. It sends a surge of tingly pleasure along every nerve ending in my upper body. I might make a small sound, not even a whole huff of air, but I can tell he feels it, because something changes in the tension of his body. If we weren't surrounded by people, I'd turn around and…

But we *are* surrounded by people, and they're all watching us with fascination.

I shake off the surge of chemical attraction, return my attention to Lucy and Rachel, expecting Clark to drop his arms. But he doesn't. He just settles me back against his big body, the two of us leaning against the deck railing, a couple just like any other.

Stop, Jessa. Stop wishing it were true.

Amanda and Hanna join us, too, just as Lucy says, "Hey. I don't want to put you on the spot, but I have a question."

"Shoot," I say. I'm hyperaware of everything about Clark's body: the wall of his chest and abs behind my head and back, the just-barely-decent cant of his hips away from my ass. I want to step in, lean back, feel it all. I want to make him have to choose between being hard against me in public or finding an excuse to run away. I want to make him uncomfortable. I want to make him lose control.

Pay! Attention!

"...could do it myself but I'm realizing I can't, not if I also want to take advantage of this opportunity..." Lucy is saying.

Wait, what?

I'm suddenly totally locked in on her.

She bites her lip. "I don't want you to have to drop or rearrange anything. I'm not asking this as a favor because you're dating my brother-in-law to be. I've just heard amazing things about your work, and if anyone's going to do my wedding who isn't me, I want it to be you. I just know I can't do both things well, the Herself account and my wedding."

Holy shit. Lucy Spiro-about-to-be-Wilder is asking me to plan her wedding. "I—I don't think—"

She gives me puppy dog eyes. If puppy dogs could have baby blues. "Please say you'll do it. I'll pay you your usual fee, plus I'll throw in a free marketing consult for your business."

"Her weddings are amazeballs!" Amanda chimes in. "I went to Petra Jacoby's, and it was killer."

"I know," Lucy says. "I hear about them all the time. And what happened with your business was criminal. Literally."

"Wait, what—?" Clark says behind me, and I have to elbow him to get him to shut up, because if we'd been dating more than a month, he would know this story.

But Lucy, Amanda, Rachel, and Hanna are no dummies.

"You don't *know*?" Lucy says, staring at Clark over my head, aghast. "You didn't *tell* him?"

Aaugh! Did I? Didn't I? Which would be more believable? Seconds tick by. It feels like an eternity. But before I can make a choice, Clark jumps in. "Oh, right! Sorry! The mess with your business. I just got confused there for a second."

Shoulders go down. Eyes swing back to me. Crisis averted.

Whew. Clark's definitely living up to my assessment of him as quick on his feet.

I shoot him a grateful glance, and one side of his mouth turns up. He gives me a slight, tight nod. *Gotchoo, babe.*

Without thinking, I cover his hand—near my waist—with mine.

He turns his hand, wraps mine up, and squeezes.

I get the head-to-toe warm fuzzies. Concentrated heavily between my legs.

Lucy puts her hand out, a pleading gesture. "I know it's a super-short timeline. To get something done by September."

"Oh, wow, September," I say, thinking, *I could just squeeze that in before I leave.* And with that and the Darman-Stevens wedding, I'd be setting Imani up for success going forward.

"It's really soon, I know, but I swear to God I won't be a bridezilla."

Okay, now. This is a hill I'll die on. "There's no such thing as a bridezilla," I say briskly. "There are only brides who know what they want, and people with unreasonable expectations that women shouldn't have opinions about their own parties."

"See?" Amanda demands. "You *have* to hire her."

Oops, just made it worse for myself. But the truth is, I'm already realizing The Best Day needs to take this wedding. For Imani and the future of her company. The Wilders—and their entourage—are well-connected enough in Rush Creek that between them and the Darman-Stevens wedding, she could totally rehabilitate the business's tarnished image. Not to mention that in all probability Rachel and Brody will need a wedding planner soon, and Imani could be in line for that job, too.

And who knows how many other Wilder weddings might follow?

Plus, I would love for Imani to be able to take Lucy up on that free marketing consult for The Best Day.

"I can't make any final decisions without talking to my partner," I tell Lucy. "But I'd like to do it. I'll get back to you in the next day or so."

Lucy nods; that's good enough for her.

"I should probably also mention—I'm moving to the East Coast in early October. So it really would have to happen in the September timeframe. Otherwise Imani Jones, who's my number two right now and will be taking over the business, will have to pick up at that point."

Every mouth on the deck falls open simultaneously. And Clark makes an abrupt move, like a man who's just felt the earth shift under his feet and is grappling for a new footing.

Oh, *shit*.

"You're—?" Clark begins.

I shake my head, and he clamps his mouth shut, getting it. There is literally no way this would be the first time he was finding out I was moving.

"You're—you're moving?"

Amanda fills the gap.

"Yeah."

Amanda looks from Clark to me and back again.

"We'll cross that bridge when we come to it," Clark says sharply, and everyone looks away.

Gabe joins us on the deck, saving us from the moment. He's a leaner and darker-haired version of Clark, his wavy locks longer but his facial hair more shadow than Clark's beard.

"Jessa's going to plan your wedding!" Amanda crows.

"I—" I begin, about to explain that I haven't actually committed yet, and can't, until I talk to Imani, but it's basically useless. I totally understand why Clark felt he had to resort to deception to get Amanda off his back.

"Awesome," Gabe says. "That'll make it super convenient for you to work with her."

He seems to be addressing Clark.

"What?" Clark asks. He releases me and steps to my side. I miss his warmth at my back.

"I've been meaning to—"

Lucy cuts in, putting a hand on Gabe's arm. "We'll leave you guys to this conversation, okay?" she says. "Come with me, ladies. Rumor has it there's chocolate cake in the kitchen."

18

CLARK

Wait, don't go! I want to call to the women, but they've gone in search of chocolate, and that's not something any man should stand in the way of. Plus, I'm charmed by their easy acceptance of Jessa—and hers of them.

But I don't want to be left alone with Gabe.

Pretty sure I know what he's going to ask me. There are so many reasons it's a bad idea—and no way out.

Also, I'm still totally reeling from what just happened. All of it. Lucy recruited Jessa to plan her wedding. And Jessa all but said she'd do it.

And Jessa's moving to the East Coast in October.

I mean, it's really the first thing that's the big deal. Jessa planning Lucy's wedding.

That's not going to make it easy to have a clean breakup. Not at all.

Jessa is going to be around. She's going to be everywhere, in all our family business.

And I don't hate the idea nearly as much as I should.

"Look," Gabe says. "I get it if what I'm about to ask is too hard for you… you won't hurt my feelings if you say no."

I shift my ruffled focus to my favorite brother. My brothers are not known for their soft-and-serious talk, and Gabe in particular is about as no-nonsense as humans come, so the fact that he's sugar-coating what he's about to say is… terrifying. Also, pretty sure the words coming out of his mouth were dictated to him by Lucy earlier today, but maybe not. It's possible he has a soft heart and a way with words he just hasn't shown us yet.

"I want you to be my best man."

There you go. That's the Gabe I know and love. Short, to-the-point, no-nonsense—and not someone you can say no to.

And I don't want to say no to him. Gabe, in his impossible, bossy, prickly way, is not only my favorite brother and—might as well own it—best friend—but the head of our family and the reason we're all gainfully employed.

If he asked me to give him my firstborn, I'd have to at least consider the request.

So being his best man?

Not much to think about.

I nod. "Of course."

He looks a little surprised, which pisses me off. "Dude. I would give you a kidney."

I'm not ready to promise the firstborn thing out loud. Knowing Gabe, he'd hold me to it. *A verbal contract is a contract, Clark*, he would say, all serious and man-of-the-family, as he snatched my child from my arms. Love Gabe, but there's nothing like inheriting a business and the responsibility for seven people's happiness when you're fifteen to kill your sense of humor.

"But about Jessa planning the wedding?" I cock my head. "You should get Luce off that train. If Jessa and I don't last it'll be a shit show."

This is me, trying to do the right thing. While meanwhile, a solid part of me (that part, yes, but not only that part) is loving the idea of an excuse to keep Jessa around. We'd have to continue to pretend to be dating at least through the wedding. I'd have scores of opportunities to put my arms around her and plant kisses on her cheek. Neck. Ear.

Mouth.

Jessa's mouth.

Jessa's fucking mouth.

He shoots me a quizzical look, probably because I've gone off to another planet, one where Jessa and I are kissing in a tent in the woods like we've completely forgotten who we are. "You guys looked pretty cozy a minute ago."

Cozy's one word for it. It was definitely *warm*, if by warm, I mean hot as hell having her slim, soft body next to mine. I had to call on vast reserves of self-control not to put us both through a repeat of my middle-of-the-night wooden spoon scenario.

"Besides," he says, pinning me with his I'm-the-boss-of-this-family dark eyes. "I know you, Clark, and you're not the type to bring a woman home to meet us if you're not pretty darn sure you're serious about her. Especially not after Emma."

That strikes me right where it hurts most, in the guilt.

"What?" he demands. "What's that look on your face?"

"I—"

Gabe frowns. "You're freaking out, aren't you."

"I'm not *freaking out*," I say.

"Yes, you are. About Emma."

About Emma? Right. He thinks... right.

"Okay, yeah, maybe I'm freaking out a little." *Although you have no idea why.*

He tips his chin at me. "I'm just going to say this once, Clark. She'd want you to be happy. You know she would." He winces at the expression on my face. "I'm sorry, man. But you know it's true. She'd be pissed if she thought you were holding back on something good because of her."

"I don't know about that. If I'd died and Emma got left behind, I don't know if I'd be a big enough man to want her to be happy."

I've had plenty of time to think about that scenario. It was all I wished for—that our situations could be reversed—for months.

Gabe squints, and his gaze softens, like he's looking off in the distance at something.

"Don't," I say.

"Don't what."

"Don't try to put yourself in my shoes. They fucking suck. Just be happy Lucy's here, okay?"

He shrugs. "Yeah. Sorry. I just—"

I hold up a hand.

"Got it," he says. "Thanks, though. For being willing to do the best man thing. It means a lot to me."

"Gabe!!" Lucy howls from inside.

"What?" he calls back.

She appears in the slider. "Buck just chewed Jessa's sweater and threw up in the living room! Come clean it up! And also, we're buying Jessa a new sweater!"

Gabe gives me a strange look.

"What?" I demand.

"Long story," he says. "If you and Jessa are still together at the wedding, I'll tell you."

Then he trots off to clean up Buck's mess.

I'm left standing there, wondering what the hell he's talking about.

19

JESSA

"You're moving," he says flatly.

We're in his truck on the way back to my place after Lucy and Gabe's engagement party. It's not super late—the party, which had started mid-afternoon, wound down around nine when the kids got squirrelly and parents rounded them up for bedtime. I'm warm and loose, cheered by the good food, excellent company, and free-flowing drinks, but the blankness of his tone yanks me back to earth.

"I'm sorry I didn't mention it sooner," I say. "I think it's because I meant to tell you in the tent when we were talking about my family, and then I fell asleep before I could say it out loud."

"I remember wondering what that garbled sentence was supposed to be," he says, shaking his head and smiling.

"My brain sort of registered that I'd said it then, and then I forgot to bring it up again, and then—there we were."

"Well," he says, shrugging. "I think we pulled it off tonight, right?"

I spin through a slideshow of the day—warm hugs, funny conversations, all the interesting people I met and interacted with. "Yeah."

We're both silent. I shiver, suddenly, and shrug myself into the remnants of the sweater that Gabe's dog, Buck, ate one sleeve of.

Clark darts a quick look my way. "They liked you." His voice is low.

I don't know how to respond. Spending this day with Clark wasn't what I thought it would be. I'd imagined it'd be stressful, keeping up the pretense. Hard work. I thought I'd be bored meeting someone's family when I didn't have any stake in the situation.

Instead, it was one of the best days I can remember having. I felt welcomed, accepted. I loved everyone I met.

And Clark?

He makes a great fake boyfriend.

He kept my drink full. He brought me food. He made sure I was introduced to everyone. He kept an eye on me, and jumped in when he thought I needed rescuing—which only happened once, when Nan, who owns Rush Creek Bakery, launched into a lengthy dissertation on why there is no way to make gluten free bread that's as good as the "real thing."

Even my insistence that Nan was preaching to the choir didn't cut her lecture any shorter. But Clark came and swooped me off to meet his cousin Arwin, who was visiting from Seattle.

As Clark pulled me out of earshot, Nan was still calling, "I challenge you to bring any gluten-free bread into the bakery and we'll do a head-to-head comparison!"

"Thank you again for saving me from Nan," I tell him.

"That's what fake boyfriends are for," he says, a smile tugging up the corner of his mouth.

"Well, you're a good one."

"My pleasure. You make the job easy."

I cast a surreptitious glance his way and find him watching me, eyes a shade darker than usual. The intensity of his look catches my breath in my chest and heats up my cheeks. I cough.

He looks away, staring straight ahead, eyes on the road, expression unreadable.

It's quiet again, just the purr of the truck's engine and the sound of wind whipping over something lashed in the flatbed. Clark asks, "Are you really going to be Lucy's wedding planner?"

I steal another glance at him. "Leaning towards it. Why? Is that an issue for you?"

"No—it's not that—it's just—" He hesitates. "Gabe asked me to be his best man."

"Yeah. I thought that might be what that whole thing was about."

He shoots me a quick, wry look. "I'm in way over my head. There's probably no guy on earth less equipped to arrange rentals of dress clothes or plan a party than I am."

"Don't panic. The Best Day has a guidebook for the best man. With checklists and everything."

"You're kidding!"

"We have guidebooks for all the major players. Helps everything run smoothly, and then no one feels crappy later when they didn't know about some wedding-day thing."

The side of his mouth closest to me turns up. "So Lucy

and Amanda are right. You're the bomb when it comes to wedding planning."

"Or something like that. Maybe something not so messy, fiery, and explosive."

He shoots me a quick glance, and there's something considering in it.

"So you're going to tell them yes. Even though you said you had to check with your partner about doing the wedding."

"She'll say yes."

"And I couldn't—wouldn't—say no to Gabe." He takes a deep breath. "So I'm thinking—would that be awkward?"

"Awkward?"

"If we broke up. And then had to keep crossing paths."

My body automatically braces itself against the words "broke up," like it would if we were actually dating, before my conscious brain kicks in and I remember that we're talking about fake dating and a fake breakup. Still, he's right: Since it's real to his family, a breakup might inject awkwardness into the wedding planning process. "I guess it could."

He pulls into the parking lot of my apartment building, and into a space. He kills the engine and sits facing straight ahead, his hands in his lap.

"Clark?" I ask.

He turns and gives me a slightly puzzled look. "Is this weird to say? I liked that everyone liked you so much. It made me happy."

Something lurches in my belly. It's the word "happy" in Clark's mouth. My being at his family's party made him *happy*. And I know by now he's not a guy who throws stuff like that around.

But as I'm casting about for the right thing to say, he adds, "I might have gotten too into it because of that. Forgot for a second that it was an act. Do you know what I mean?"

He turns to look at me. I don't know what he's asking or how to answer. And I'm hyperaware that Clark's being totally real with me. That feeling I had—that Clark and I are friends, it's back. I don't want to screw this up.

"Nah," I say. "It wasn't weird. You did great. And I probably got a little too into it, too. I think it just happens. Like actors, in a play. They forget they're acting and start feeling all the things, and next thing you know, they're dating. But it doesn't last in real life because the feelings were never real. They were never that compatible, when it comes down to it."

I'm talking really fast. Trying to get us back on normal footing.

And I think I know the best, most efficient way to do that.

"It might be easier..." I begin.

He picks his big hands up and puts them on the steering wheel at ten and two, like he's holding on for comfort.

"...if we just called it now," I finish.

Breath gusts out of Clark. Like he's been holding it. "Yeah," he says, nodding. "That's what I was thinking, too."

You know at the beach, when a wave is rolling back out, and then another one comes in, and they smash into each other? That's how I feel right now. Relief and disappointment, one rolling in, one rolling out, and I'm not sure which is coming and which is going.

"Okay," I say. "We'll just tell them that we realized it was too soon for you. Too soon for both of us," I add quickly, thinking of lying in the tent and listening to Reuben and Corinna. "And we wanted to be able to stay friends and work on the wedding together without having it all go to shit. That part's completely true. They'll buy that, right?"

Clark's quiet a minute. Then he says, "Yeah."

I wait for him to say something else, but he doesn't, and after a moment, I say, "So we have a plan?"

He takes a deep breath. I turn to look at him, and he turns to look back. For a long, suspended moment, I feel a weird, unlikely, unwanted surge of hope. Then he nods. "Yes," he says decisively. "We have a plan."

This time, I recognize the disappointment.

20

CLARK

Are you free? Lucy texts me.
Basically? Doing Wilder office work, but nothing critical.
Can you drive Jessa to Edelweiss?
What's Edelweiss?
My phone rings.

"Edelweiss is a wedding venue. *The* Rush Creek wedding venue. It has a last-minute September cancellation, but the invitations are at the printer, literally in the queue, so I have to decide asap." She's talking a mile a minute. I can barely understand her, but I get the gist.

"And you and Gabe are in Portland."

"Right. And I never actually *saw* the place because they told me they were booked out till next year. I need Jessa over there to grab video for me and put down the deposit before their manager goes home at four, but I just called her and her car battery's dead and roadside assistance told her 90 minutes minimum. Can you drive her?"

The sound of Jessa's name—or really, the thought of

being in the same vehicle with her again—sends a rush of blood through my veins. Almost two weeks have passed without my seeing her, which is probably—definitely—for the best. We're now officially through with the fake dating.

And yet, I still haven't told my family about the "breakup."

Yeah. I know. Not my finest work.

There have been several moments when it would have made perfect sense for me to fess up. Like when Rachel asked me how things were going with Jessa and I said, "Fine!" Or when Hanna asked whether Jessa was going to be my plus-one at the wedding, and instead of saying, *No, actually, we broke up*, I said, "I mean, if we're still together when the invitations go out." Both of which are basically the adult equivalent of crossing your fingers while lying to your mom.

Jessa thinks we fake broke up, and Lucy thinks we're still fake together, and if I'm not careful one of them is going to tell the other the fake story they believe, and then it's going to get confusing for everyone.

Jessa will want to know why I didn't do what we agreed to do, and I will not have a good answer for her.

I hum. "You know what? I just realized I have to—I have this marketing email that should go out this afternoon. Is Amanda free?"

"Amanda's got a big job tonight and she's in the kitchen," Lucy says. "Heath and Connor are at work, Brody and Rachel are out in the boat with a group. Barb's meeting the Kenning kids after school. Kane's getting his teeth cleaned. Hanna's doing a leadership training course."

I can hear Lucy's voice getting smaller and higher, like a toy wound too tight.

"Which marketing email?" she demands.

Busted.

In the background, I can hear Gabe's voice saying, "What's the problem?"

"Um, you know what? The email can go out tomorrow morning."

Lucy lets out a breath so big I can hear it whooshing against the phone's mic. "Thank you. I'll tell her you're coming."

"No! That's okay! I'll tell her."

There's a fractional hesitation on the other end that tells me my weird behavior has been detected. Why am I surrounded by women with mind-reading powers? It's like living among superheroes.

"Clark?" Lucy asks.

"Mmm-hmm," I say.

"Everything okay with you?"

"Hunky dory."

"Because if there were anything you wanted to talk about with me, you know you could, right?"

"Of course."

There's another long pause. Then she says, "Bring a bathing suit."

"What?"

"One of the reasons Edelweiss is my number one is that it has hot springs right on the premises. The tour includes a soak. I figured you and Jessa would definitely want to take advantage."

"I—"

"The springs are supposedly beautiful. And super romantic."

Right. There is no earthly reason why any man would

turn down an opportunity to sit in a hot spring with a beautiful woman he is supposedly dating.

"Got it," I say.

And here's the thing. I don't want to turn down an opportunity to sit in a hot spring with Jessa. I want to see Jessa in a bathing suit with droplets of water clinging to her shoulders and steam rising off her skin.

I want to lick the fucking droplets off her shoulders.

The Venus in my mental movie reaches up to where her bikini strings are tied at the base of her neck and unties them. The strings drop, and—

"Thank you again, Clark. You're my hero today."

"No problem," I say.

I set the phone down and drop my head into my hands.

This is bliss.

I mean, in a perfect world, you wouldn't be able to smell the sulfur, but to be honest, I got used to it really fast.

I'm sitting on a rock ledge, sunk chest-deep in mineral-rich 104-degree water.

The hot springs occurred naturally, but Edelweiss built expensive and beautiful landscaping around them. Rock outcroppings and walls ring and divide the expanse of blue-green water. I'm in a small grotto, surrounded by flowers and vines and trees.

The water feels so good. I hadn't realized how sore my body was from the most recent wilderness trip. Being sore after a trip is just background noise to me at this point, but when I lowered myself into the steaming water, it was like letting go of a heavy burden.

The proprietor of Edelweiss, whose name is Lewis Raglan, gave us a detailed tour, which finished up here. He handed us keys to the dressing rooms and told us we could enjoy an hour in the springs before he had to close up, and that we should head back inside when we were done and dressed.

Jessa steps out from the dressing area and into view. She's wearing a white terry-cloth cover-up with a zipper up the front. My fingers twitch from wanting to grasp the zipper and tug it down.

She does it herself, unselfconsciously undressing like she knows exactly how good she looks. Which is really fucking good.

Her bikini is black-and-white checker boards, the tiny kind —like your grandma's curtains, except that Jessa definitely doesn't look like anyone's grandma. The upper curves of her small but upright breasts are exposed. The bottom is a tiny triangle with a ruffle on either side, a combination of flirty and sexy that makes my mouth dry. Out of her clothes, Jessa's body is gorgeous. Narrow waist, flared hips, and an innie belly-button that I want to dip my tongue into—on my way lower.

She drops the white coverup on the stone surface of the grotto. If she were scripting this to drive me nuts, she couldn't do any better.

Easing into the water, she lets out a soft "eep" sound when her feet make contact with the water. I want to beg her not to hide all that satiny bare skin under the water—but I don't have the right.

She's my fake girlfriend that I broke up with.

Is the regret I'm feeling right now fake or real?

I roll my eyes at myself.

"Ohh," she groans, sinking lower.

I'm glad I'm submerged. Swim trunks tell all the truths. Unlike me, apparently.

She dunks to her chin, then pop backs up and settles herself onto the ledge across from me.

Just like in my fantasy, her skin sparkles with droplets of water, and steam rises off her.

I want to tell her she's wrecking me.

I should have known better than to think I could keep a lid on this attraction. You don't want someone the way I want Jessa and play it cool. It will leak out around the edges, demand to be seen and heard, until your choices are: walk away or dive in.

Which is it, Clark Wilder? Which is it?

Jessa crosses her arms over her chest and fixes me with a look. "Clark," she says sternly.

Uh-oh.

"Is it my imagination, or does Lucy not think we're broken up?"

I close my eyes. Not because I'm hoping she'll disappear if I'm looking, but because I'm hoping to come up with a brilliant explanation for my omission.

Nope.

"I, uh, didn't tell her."

"Did you tell everyone else?" she asks. She doesn't sound mad. Just confused.

"I meant to, but I've been busy with trips. It's our summer season. And I was planning the bachelor and bachelorette parties with Amanda. I—I'm sorry. I just didn't get to it."

She stares at me. "You *didn't get to it.*"

Still, I don't think she's mad. Just... curious.

Moment of truth.

"I meant to," I confess. "I tried to. I just—I couldn't."

"You *couldn't.*"

I rake my hand through my hair, then drop it to my side, where it drops into the water with a faint splash that sends out another round of ripples. "I didn't want to not be fake dating you."

"Clark," she says sternly. "I can't understand that sentence. It's a double negative. With a 'fake' thrown in, just to make it more confusing. You're going to have to spell it out for me."

Dive in, something deep inside me urges.

"I think we should keep it going until the wedding," I say.

"What?"

"The fake dating. I think we should keep going till the wedding. Otherwise, there's going to be so much bullshit with plus ones and the invitations and everything. This will keep it super simple."

She tilts her head to one side, scowling. "I'm really not so sure about super simple. Lucy and Amanda invited me to girls' night out next Wednesday night. It was pretty obvious from the subtext that they're rolling the welcome mat out for me because I'm dating you. The longer this goes on, the more I get tangled up with your family and friends, and the more complicated it'll be to untangle at the end."

"You can stay friends with them," I tell her.

She frowns. "Clark." She's pissed. I can't really blame her.

"We agreed. We got Reuben off my back and your mom off yours. We came up with an exit strategy, and we were going to escape the whole thing unscathed. That never happens, you know. There's, like, a whole romance trope devoted to exploring how fake dating *always* causes trouble. You always get caught. It's always a hot mess, but we had a chance to get off scot free. So please, enlighten me: *What the fuck?*"

Her arms are crossed. Her brows are drawn together. She's completely fucking adorable.

Slowly, I rise from my stone seat. I push through the hot water until I'm directly in front of her.

Her eyes are huge, and even in the low light of our forest nest, I can see how big her pupils are. The swim trunks, as predicted, are poor armor, and her gaze drops. Her lower lip softens, and her top teeth find it, digging into the soft flesh. On a small exhale, her legs part, making room for me to kneel between them.

I bend down and kiss her.

21

JESSA

Clark's mouth. Holy fuck.

He kisses like he's been starving for it, and it's such a rush, being wanted like that. Being needed like that. I give right back. Our mouths are slick and steamy and I can't tell where I end and he starts. Or who's making the small, desperate sounds and the rough grunts of need. My legs part, making room for him to crowd close. His big hands find my hips and draw me forward on the bench, bringing my sex flush against his erection. The moan is definitely mine. He swallows it and draws another one out of me with a rock of his hips, a stroke of heat and friction. I feel like my blood's the same temperature as the water.

Someone clears their throat behind me, and Clark leaps back like he's been stung.

"Sorry to interrupt," Lew—Edelweiss's owner—says sheepishly. Lew is a tall, lean, middle-aged man with flyaway hair and a thick old-school mustache. "I didn't realize you two were *together*."

Neither did we. I lift my fingertips to my tingling lips, then quickly drop them.

Lew frowns. "I'm so sorry to do this—but I just got a call that I need to pick my wife up in Bend in forty-five minutes. I'm the last one here, so I need to let you two out and close up."

"Oh, gosh, of course!" I say.

"Take your time," Lew says, before backing out of the grotto with another apologetic smile.

Clark and I don't look at each other as we hoist ourselves out of the water and retreat to two side-by-side dressing rooms. I hear the sound of board shorts rustling, which means he's now naked. And—odds are—still hard. I don't quite stifle a moan at the thought.

"Jessa?" His voice drifts through the wooden wall between us.

"It was a bad time for an interruption," I whisper. "I was enjoying myself."

Sometimes honesty is the best policy.

He groans. "Jesus, Jessa. Fuck. Yes."

I take a deep breath. "So does this mean we're fake dating but real kissing?"

He's quiet for a moment. Then he says, "Would that work for you?"

I wish I could say that I took a long time to think about the question. Or its potential consequences. But really, it's not the kind of question you *think* about. It's a feeling question, and I am full to the brim with feelings, still branded from lips to knees with the sensation of his kiss and the press of his body. I just want him to kiss me again.

"Yes."

I can hear the sound of towel on skin—Edelweiss has

provided us with very thick, soft bath sheets—and clothing rustling. I strip my bathing suit off, noting what that one intense kiss did to my body. My nipples are cool points, my sex already molten for him.

I dry off and get dressed. I step out of my dressing room a moment before he exits his. "We should get out of here so Lew can get where he needs to be."

He nods. His eyes are hot and curious on me. I want to grab him and pull him back in. I want to sink into the heat between us.

Side by side, in silence, we head inside. We thank Lew, who walks us out to the parking lot, climbs into his Subaru, and drives off. Clark's truck is the only vehicle left in the lot.

Clark doesn't start the engine right away. He sits, facing straight ahead, hands tight on the wheel. I stew in the passenger seat, full of feelings I don't know what to do with, and quite a few I'm completely clear on. I want more of that kissing. I want to know what's in his head. I want to understand what's in mine. I toy with the possibility of suggesting that we take this conversation somewhere else, but part of me is afraid that if we walk away now, we'll never have it. Besides, the lot is hemmed in by trees. It's still light out, but because of the woods, it feels very private.

"Just kissing?" He says it so conversationally that it's a tease. A stroke of one finger down the sensitive skin of my inner thigh.

I shiver. "I mean, I do *really* like kissing. So it could be just kissing."

"Well, yeah. Kissing's great. We can definitely do lots of it. Just trying to figure out the, um, *rules*. Of this. Fake dating. Real kissing."

I take a deep breath. "Not just kissing," I say. "There could also be..." I hesitate. "There could be touching."

He draws a quick breath in the quiet of the truck. My own breath hitches to match.

"Touching where?" he asks quietly.

"Everywhere," I whisper back.

"Real touching, everywhere," he murmurs, like he's taking notes. "And licking?"

"Definitely licking."

We're both breathing hard.

"About the licking," he says, his voice a husky tease. "Is that also *everywhere*?"

"I guess—I'd leave that up to you?" I squeak.

"If it were up to me"—his voice is like rough velvet now, over every nerve ending in my body—"I would say yes. Definitely yes. But not all at once. A little bit at a time. Working my way down. Stopping in places. Paying attention where attention needed to be paid. Also, I'd throw in nipping and pinching and twisting and—oh, why the hell not. Sucking."

It's like a tsunami of good words, each one molasses slow and rough in his mouth, rolling over me; I press my thighs together, but it doesn't help. It doesn't bring any satisfaction at all.

"Jessa," he says.

"Mmm-hmm?"

"You're squirming."

"Mmm-hmm."

"Real squirming?"

"Clark." I can't keep the begging out of my voice.

"Get over here," he says roughly, and I get.

22

CLARK

She makes a small, almost wounded, sound.

I reach both hands out to her, helping her scramble around the center console, lifting her into my lap. Before I have time to relish the feel of her thighs, the sudden weight of her body, the press of her groin against my erection, her mouth is on mine, soft and eager.

Kissing Jessa is different from kissing other women.

It's so fucking satisfying. Like, obviously, I want more. I'm a typical penis-owner, and that thing is insatiable. Extra so with Jessa because she turns me on so much.

But in this case, I also want to just let it happen. Savor it.

These are long, deep kisses. Luxury kisses. We're tasting each other, breathing each other in. We're getting to know pace and angle and pressure. Meanwhile, our bodies are moving together, wanting more, but it's not urgent. It's slow, like we're still moving under the steaming surface of the springs, through water.

It's so fucking hot.

She's so fucking hot.

She's restless in my lap. "Shh," I say. "Slow down. I'll get you there. Trust me."

She whimpers. I kiss her again, savoring the way she gives right back, matching me. Opening to me, but not passively. Meeting the thrust of my tongue with the thrust of hers, notching up my neediness. I cup my hands behind her head, holding it, and she leans back into my palms, totally trusting. I kiss her whole mouth, then her upper lip. I draw its softness into my mouth, nip and suckle. Then the other lip, and she moans and rocks herself against me. Going slow will require all my self-control, but the feeling of riding this edge is worth it.

I drop little kisses all over her face—lips, nose, eyelids. I skate my mouth along her cheek, loving the huff of breath she makes, then find her ear, each of its curves. She makes a different sound—a soft gasp—and shivers, arching. I bury my face there in the silk of her hair, breathing in lavender and vanilla and the smell of her skin, concentrated. I can smell her arousal, drifting to me like the scent of the ocean, and I have to count to ten and think about how much I hate paperwork until I can stick to the plan. *Slow.*

She wants more. She's rocking against me, rubbing her breasts against my chest, clutching my arms to get the leverage she craves.

"It's better slow." I hold her steady. I grip her hips, stopping their pleading motion. "You know I'm right, don't you?"

She struggles against my hold, groans her frustration. "Not *fair*," she says.

"But you know I'm right."

"I know you're *hard*."

"I am," I agree. "I want to bury myself in you. I want to fill you up until you scream my name. But that's not what's going to happen right now."

"What's... going... to... happen?" she asks breathlessly.

"We're going to kiss some more. A lot more. And it's going to feel so good. All that kissing, all that wanting. You're going to want it so bad, you think you can't stand it. You'll think you're going to come without even being touched. You're going to be right there, riding the edge. And then—and only then—I'm going to make you come."

She moans. I'm glad we're locked, alone, in the silent truck, because that moan would definitely penetrate apartment walls and carry across forest groves. It's deep and needy, and I feel it all the way to the root of my cock and the base of my spine.

"I want that," she whimpers. "I want the part where you bury yourself and I scream your name."

"You'll get it," I tell her. "But in the meantime, kiss me."

She does. Her mouth is helplessly open, soft and wet; all her rhythm and technique is shot to hell, and I love it. It's the way I know she'll be when I'm inside her, lost and abandoned to pure pleasure.

We kiss and kiss like that, surfing sensation, oblivious to everything else. I'm completely tuned into her, and it feels so fucking good. Her mouth under mine, her hands tugging my shirt out of my jeans, sliding up my overheated skin, a wash of cool pleasure. I don't think I've ever been this hard in my life. Finding the bottom of her t-shirt, I slide my hands under the fabric. Her skin is softer than I could have guessed. I ghost my hands over her ribs, cup the curves I've been dying to palm. I find her nipples through the flimsy lace of her bra, tease them to hard, needy points.

She curses me, breathless, and I capture the dirty words against my tongue, urging her on with my mouth, flicking and teasing her with my fingers.

"I'm... there," she pants. "Riding... the edge."

"I know," I murmur against her ear. I rock under her. Once. Twice.

One more thrust, one more pinch of both nipples, a long, slick slide of my tongue against hers, and I tip her over.

Her hips bear down hard on me. She pushes her breasts into my palms. She bites my mouth so hard I gasp.

She rides it out on my cock, through the layers of our clothing, rough and relentless and mindless, murmuring my name over and over again. I'm so hard it hurts. Tension winds itself tight in my low belly. I jerk against her, grip her hips too hard. I'm going to go over with her if I'm not careful.

She knows exactly how close I am, too. When her eyes flicker back open, after she smiles sleepily at me, her smile turns taunting. "How does it feel now, Mr. Self Control?"

I grin at her.

"Good," I say. "Really fucking good."

23

JESSA

Wow.

Okay.

That was...

That was the good stuff.

I hope there is more of that where that came from. Because a girl could definitely get used to it.

I reach for the button of Clark's hiking pants, but he stalls my hand there. "It doesn't have to be tit-for-tat," he says. "There's a statistic about the number of lifetime orgasms that men and women have, and you're almost guaranteed to have a deficit. So you can just accept this one as your due."

I touch my palm to his cheek, and he tilts his head so that his beard settles against my skin. It's a lovely feeling. "I want this," I say. "I want to touch you."

He makes a gruff sound of assent and lets my hand go.

I unbutton and unzip him, freeing him. He's pretty, which I know isn't a word we use for penises a lot, but I swear. Thick and symmetrical and straight, the skin a consistent, dusky red-brown. I wrap my hand around him. The head of his cock is swollen and slick with pre-cum, and he groans at my touch.

"It won't take much," he warns, and leans forward to reach for a tissue, which he hands me.

He's right. It doesn't. Just a few long strokes of my fist, my thumb shimmying over that slick head, and then a few hard, jerky thrusts of his hips while I hold my fist still for him. I don't use the tissue. I duck my head and catch the pearls of cum against my lips and tongue and swallow them down, and he makes a rough, anguished noise at the sight. I make a matching sound at the feel of his cock throbbing hard against my hand, and the silkiness of his taut skin against my lips. Another day, I want all of this in my mouth.

I pop off—audibly, with a last tidying swirl of my tongue—and tell him that.

"Fuck," he pants. "Fuck. Jessa."

We clean up and tuck in and sit for a minute. I steal a glance at him. He steals one back and our eyes meet. We both smile.

Something sharp and beautiful rises up in me.

"I like real kissing," Clark says conversationally.

"I like real kissing, too."

When Clark smiles for real, I can see that his eye teeth are a little crooked. That he has a deep dimple, but only in one cheek. That he has a starburst of smile lines at the corners of both eyes.

"Clark," I say helplessly.

"What?"

"Nothing."

He sweeps my face with his gaze, then accepts that's all he's getting for now. He starts the truck's engine.

I reach out to turn on the radio, and he lunges for me, swatting my hand away.

"What the—?" I demand. We wrestle for control, and I succeed in jabbing the power button. "Save Your Tears" by The Weekend comes on, and I hoot, delighted. "Seriously, Clark? The big, bad Mountain Man listens to KILY? All love songs, all the time?"

He's actually blushing. "Amanda turned it on the last time she was in my truck?"

"You are so fucking full of it! It wasn't Amanda! It was you!"

"I may or may not have a soft spot for cheesy pop," he admits.

I am so delighted I can't contain myself. "'All of Me' by John Legend?" I ask.

He wrinkles up his face apologetically and nods.

"Ed Sheeran's 'Shape of You'?"

Another nod. And then, "'My Heart Will Go On,'" he confesses.

I howl. "Oh, my God, Clark, if this gets out!"

He crosses his arms, suddenly fierce. "You can't tell anyone!"

"They don't know," I say. It's not a question. "Your brothers don't know."

He hangs his head, like his dirty secret is about a kinky thing for pigeons and not cheesy love songs. And I have to admit, I'm guessing the Wilder brothers are more likely to tear one of their own to shreds over sappy pop than over pigeonphilia.

"Gah! Clark! How have you managed not to get caught

before now? How am I the one to finally learn your dark secret?"

He gives me a fierce look. "It might have something to do with the way you disarmed me right beforehand. Not a lot of living brain cells left after that hand job. Or blow job."

"Hybrid," I offer, fighting back a smile.

"Jesus, Jessa, that was hot. Not gonna be able to get that one of my head for a good long time. Currently in slot one in the spank bank. No, wait. Two. Slot one is you coming on my lap." He sighs. "You bit me." He touches a finger to his lower lip and looks surprisingly happy about it.

"Sorry not sorry?" I hazard.

I'm a warm fuzzball right now. It's too much. Clark as a cheesy love song junkie, Clark telling me the top two spots in his personal spank bank are occupied by me. Clark smiling with his finger to his lip like he's urging me to keep a secret... Be still my heart. I can't take it.

"Your secret is safe with me," I say. "Unless I can use it to my advantage, in which case I plan to do that at my earliest possible convenience."

Clark glares. "Blackmail is illegal." But the corner of his mouth betrays him, crooking.

"I guess." I shrug. I can't stop smiling. "But in good news for you, I do accept sexual favors in lieu of cash."

His laugh—the one I've surprised out of him—catches me in my chest, like a swift, warm hug from someone you weren't quite sure even liked you.

24

CLARK

It's thirty-six hours after our sizzling hot encounter in the truck, and I haven't heard from her.

Of course she hasn't heard from me either.

Best case scenario, we're both playing it a tiny bit cool.

Worst case...?

She meant it to be a one-time thing. Or she thought I wanted it to be a one-time thing.

I mean, maybe it should be.

But holy fuck, I don't want it to be. I want more. More of everything. More of her mouth open for my tongue, and her lips wrapped around the head of my cock, her nipples against my palms, her back arched, her face wrecked with pleasure.

More of those moments afterwards, when she teased and I laughed.

I'd forgotten about laughing. About how good it feels when you're not faking it, even a little.

In an effort to convince myself that I can take it or leave it (patent bullshit), I decide to inventory my personal camping equipment, which is why I'm literally sharpening my knives when my doorbell rings.

Always a good look.

I set the knife down, wipe oil off my hands, and hurry to the door. Best guess? My mom with fresh-baked cookies, Gabe with some piece of equipment I need to repair, or a Jehovah's Witness with salvation on offer.

But of course it's her. Standing in my doorway, wearing yet another of those dresses that beg me to slide the straps off her shoulders.

Holding out a book.

Wait, a book?

She smiles at me, as she shows me the cover.

"I had it in my bag at Edelweiss," she says. "But somehow I forgot to give it to you. Not sure what distracted me." Her look is a frank tease, and heat washes down my body and pools, with excellent growth potential, in my dick.

I take the book: *The Best Groomsman: The Best Day's Guide to Your Wedding Role*. I set it on the hall table behind me. I take her face in my hands and kiss her. *Missed you*, I mean to say, but it comes out more like, *Holy shit, Jessa, I missed you so goddamn much*. Like, zero-to-tongues and panting in about three seconds. I've got her backed up against the door, my leg wedged between hers, before I can catch hold of my self-control.

She doesn't seem to mind so much.

Definitely not when I kneel. Or tug down her panties. Or loop one of her legs over my shoulder.

"Clark," she breathes.

"You smell so fucking good."

"Clark." It's a plea now.

"This okay?" My lips, set against the soft hair on her mound, blowing through the strands.

"God. Yes."

I tease her with cool puffs of air, then warm, until she's hitching her hips to my mouth, begging with her body. I run my thumbs along the seam of her sex, opening her to me.

I tilt my head up. "I take direction well," I say. "If it's not working for you, tell me what would, okay?"

"It's working for me," she groans, which makes my cock surge against the constraint of my boxer briefs and jeans. Then, "You didn't take direction well in your truck."

"Yeah, well, sometimes I need to be completely in charge. You can tell me if you don't like that, too."

"You haven't done anything yet I don't like," she whispers.

I go back to work, except it's not work at all. It's all soft, silky, wet flesh against my tongue and lips, and the hard nub of her clit begging to be flicked and circled and sucked. I can't decide which I love more, the soft or the swollen-hard, savoring her or pleasuring her. So I take it all and do it all, and she shifts and squirms and tries (mostly unsuccessfully) not to close her thighs on my head, which delights me.

I give her two fingers to ride, and a few moments later, she comes on a long, flat, slow, thick-tongued circle, collapsing back against the wall with a cry.

I stand up and we put her back together, and then she's on her knees in front of me.

I start to protest, and she says, "Shut up, Clark." So I do.

This is hybrid, too, her fist clutching and releasing and sliding at the base of my cock, her mouth hot on the head. It doesn't take long—getting her off gets me close, my cock full and taut-skinned and greedy—but I try to make it last as long as I can, putting my hand over hers and squeezing tight to give myself a precious few extra seconds in the heat of her mouth. Then I'm coming, hard, long pulls of from-the-toes pleasure, as she urges me on with her tongue.

My turn to lean on the wall. And then slide down it.

She sits down next to me, and then, making my heart lurch in my chest, tilts her head to rest it on my shoulder.

I lift one boneless arm to cup her silky-headed hair in my hand.

She lets out a tiny, barely audible sigh of contentment that threads through my veins like an after-shot of pleasure.

"You want—?" I attempt, but there aren't many living brain cells in there. "You want something to drink? I feel like I should offer you a cigarette."

"God, not that," she says. "But I wouldn't say no to a glass of water. And... maybe a mirror so I can check my hair?"

We stagger to our feet and I show her the bathroom, then head into the kitchen to grab us two glasses of ice water. I take them into the living room and set them on my coffee table.

And suddenly am painfully aware of my surroundings.

Nothing has changed in two years. It's all—

Emma.

The art on the wall: A poster from the Rush Creek garden tour from four years ago. One from a museum of children's book art, featuring a beautiful watercolor of Snow White. A wooden, hand-painted sign that says, "Light dispels darkness. Wisdom dispels ignorance."

The decor: Throw pillows on the couch—one with pompoms! A hand-blown vase with swirls of blues and greens.

Fucking beautiful, but I would have spent the money on equipment. Or a better coffee maker.

And the photographs on the wall behind the couch. My mom asked if I wanted her to take them down. I growled at her like a wounded animal in a trap, and she never asked again.

There's a small, soft sound from behind me and I turn to find Jessa there. Her gaze sweeps the room, finding it all: art, pillows, vase, photographs. I see the moment when it registers, on the photos.

Me and Emma. Emma and me. Emma, me, and my siblings. Emma and my mom, beaming at each other. Emma and Amanda and Heath and the kids.

"Jessa—" I say.

Her expression is blank. I can't read anything in it.

"My mother and sister have been saying for months I should put some of these away. That it would be awkward if I brought someone back here—"

She's shaking her head. Hard. "No, Clark, no. Don't be ridiculous. You absolutely shouldn't feel like you have to do that because of me. She was—she was Emma, and this is—" She gestures to indicate what she means by this. Us, together, in the front hallway, not patient enough to make it to the living room. The words draw even more lines around what's happening between us. Casual. Real kissing, fake dating. *This.*

"This is just until the wedding. It's just—what it is."

"Right," I say. I'm confused by how I feel, like I want to argue with her, even though there's nothing to argue.

Her expression softens into something tender.

"And honestly, Clark, there's no reason you have to take

them down, now or ever. Anyone who can't understand that isn't worth inviting home. Maybe someday you'll want to put some of them away, or maybe you won't. But either way, if and when you're ready to take them down, you'll take them down."

Something chokes me, high up in my chest, so I can't get words around it. *Anyone who can't understand that isn't worth inviting home.*

It's her total acceptance. Of me, exactly as I am, not some healed and perfect specimen.

"Thank you," I manage.

Her lips move, twist. A wry smile. Then she smiles for real—though it doesn't quite reach her eyes.

"You're welcome," she says. "I do give good head, don't I?"

And there it is, again, surprising me:

My laugh.

25

JESSA

"I have a confession," Amanda says.

We're sitting in Oscar's Saloon and Grille. It's girls' night out with Amanda, Lucy, Rachel, and Hanna.

I have to admit that even though spending time with Clark's sister and her posse adds a layer of complication to my already complicated dating-not-dating life, I am excited to be with them. I haven't had a group of girlfriends since the book club I was in with Emma fell apart.

"No confessions," Hanna said. "I think that's in the ground rules."

Puzzled, I look from one of them to the other, until Lucy says, "Hanna has ground rules for girls' nights out. Han, I've lost track, can you enlighten us?"

"No talking about clothes, makeup, streaming series based off romance novels, reality television, jewelry, or nylon stockings. Oh, and no one is allowed to start a sentence with 'My therapist says'—"

"I should have stayed home," Amanda groans.

"—or use the word 'bae' unironically."

"Or, apparently, confess anything," Lucy appends.

"Point of order," Rachel says.

We all look at her. Out of everyone here, she's the one I can most see becoming friends with. Down to earth, no nonsense, and a minimum of difficult-to-remember rules. "Now that Amanda has said she has something to confess, we have to let her confess it. I mean, otherwise, it's like when someone says, 'Oh, my God, I have something totally amazing to tell you. Oh, wait, no—I'm not supposed to tell anyone.'"

Hanna frowns. "I guess?"

Rachel turns to me. "Oddly enough, sex toys are exempt from the forbidden topics, which is great for me because I sell them."

I tilt my head. "You said no streaming shows made from romance novels? What about romance novels themselves? Because I read them."

I learned early on that it's best to lay that on the line upfront. I don't need women friends who are going to shame me for my book choices.

Hanna waves her hands, dismissing the possibility. "Oh, shit, no. Look. I haven't had sex with another actual human in, like, two years. Book boyfriends and sex toys. That's what I've got."

"Two *years?*" Amanda gasps. "And I thought it was bad when I had to move to counting months instead of weeks."

Hanna shrugs again. "Other people are overrated."

Amanda shakes her head, crosses her hands in an X, and makes a three-strikes buzzer noise. "Oh, hell, no, they're not. You need to get out there, babe. We need to work on that."

Hanna rolls her eyes. "New rule. No 'working on Hanna.'"

"Hey," Rachel says sharply. I get the feeling she's the person in a meeting who brings things back to the topic at hand. Me, too, so I appreciate that. "Can we return to the topic of Amanda's confession?"

We cannot, apparently, because just then, our server arrives. She's super familiar but I don't think we've met.

"Jill!" Amanda sings to the petite brunette with big blue eyes and a wide smile who has just docked at our table. "Let's seeeeee itttt!"

The "it" in question is, it turns out, a very large diamond on Jill's ring finger, which, blushingly, she extends over the table.

"So?" Amanda demands. "Tell us!"

"I thought I was going to lose my *mind*," Jill says. "He got the new job, and still no proposal. He bought the house and we moved in together, and *still* no proposal. And then I finally did it. Sent myself flowers."

Amanda's eyes get huge. "It *worked*?"

"I wish I'd listened to you sooner! I sent myself this huge bunch of flowers, and I did exactly what you said. No card. So when he asked who they were from, I said, 'there was no card.'"

"Perfect," Amanda says approvingly. My first impulse is to be judgy about the partial lie—until I remember I'm a lie wrapped in the truth wrapped in a lie, out to dinner with the very people I agreed to deceive. Yup. No judgment here. Stretch that truth, girl.

"Three days later, he picks me up from work, drives me to the airport with a bag packed in the trunk, flies us to Utah, drives us to North Rim of the Grand Canyon, and proposes at sunset."

"Oooh," Rachel says. "Nice one. I hope you told him you had to think about it for, like, a year and a half."

Jill grins. "Ha! Totally. I mean, he knew I was just giving him a hard time. And he actually apologized. He said he'd been waiting until he could afford the ring he really wanted without borrowing. He said he wanted me to have everything I deserved and he didn't want to put the rest of our life together at financial risk to get it for me."

"That's sweet," Lucy says.

"Basically, the day I sent myself the flowers was the day he brought home the paycheck that put him over the edge."

"Awww," Amanda says. "You know what? Sometimes real life is more romantic than fiction." She gets a faraway look on her face, and I make a mental note to ask her what that's about. Or maybe I'll ask Rachel, because I should probably not get into trading secrets with Amanda. I bet she's a secret shark.

"By the way," Jill says suddenly, homing in on me. "I'm Jill Cooper. I went to school with Amanda's big brother Gabe. You're the wedding guru, right?"

My turn to blush. "Guru is a strong word! Jessa Olsen." I extend my hand, and we shake.

"She's a wedding *genius*," Amanda informs Jill. "She's doing Lucy's! You should have her do yours."

"I'm moving," I remind Amanda.

She raises an eyebrow. "That's what Lucy said. And Rachel. Right before they fell madly in love with a Wilder brother and settled in Rush Creek for all eternity."

Lucy and Rachel exchange amused—and fond—looks.

"No, I mean, I'm really moving. To the Philly area to be near my sibling, who's having a baby with their boyfriend."

Amanda sighs. "We'll let you stick to that story for now."

Jill takes our drinks order, and then, since we're ready, our appetizer and food order.

When she's gone, Rachel says, "Seriously, Amanda, if you don't finish the confession, I'm going to strangle you."

"Oh, right," Amanda says. She turns to me. "I was just going to confess that when Clark first told me you guys were dating, I didn't believe him. I thought he was doing that fake dating thing that Brody always told him he should do. But then I saw you guys together at the engagement party. And no one can fake the way he was looking at you. Especially not Clark."

My breath hitches. I open my mouth, intending to say…

Something.

I don't know what.

I close my mouth again. I don't have to fake the pink rising in my cheeks. Or how flustered I feel.

A lie wrapped in the truth wrapped in a lie. Yep, that's just about the shape of it.

Seeing Emma's apartment forced me to admit to myself that fooling around with Clark caused me to catch feelings.

So I guess the photos were good. A stern reminder of where I stand. Fake dating, real kissing.

Keep the lines sharp, and you won't get hurt.

They're all smiling at me, reading my flustered expression as something else. Acknowledgement of what Amanda's saying.

"On that note," Lucy says, reaching out a hand and

covering mine with hers. "I want you to come to Vegas with us."

"What?"

"The bachelor and bachelorette parties, as I know you know, are happening next weekend in Vegas. I want you to be there, too. We're bunking up in a couple of adjacent rooms, girls and guys separate, to get the whole bachelor/bachelorette experience."

"You can share mine," Hanna says with a shrug.

I think my chin hits the table.

"If you follow the rules," she amends, but her eyes are kind.

Especially in light of the unexpected invitation from Hanna, I'm dying to say yes, but every sensible bone in my body screams no.

"I can't do that," I tell Lucy as gently as I can. "I'm not even in the wedding party."

"You're the wedding planner! That makes you part of the party. And you're with Clark." Her expression tilts, mischievous. "You know he wants you there!"

I don't know any such thing. A bachelor in Vegas with his brothers? It's heaven for a single guy, right? But I can't exactly say that out loud, since Clark is not supposed to be single at the moment. "Maybe he just wants a guy's weekend." That's the best I can do without making it weird.

Lucy is tap-tap-tapping on her phone. She sets it down and pushes it aside.

"I really appreciate the invitation," I tell her. "I really do. But I think—I think it would make it weird for everyone."

"Not for us," Lucy says, and all three women nod in agreement.

Despite the situation, I feel a surge of gratitude for their easy acceptance of me. If this is the bonus that comes with being attached to a Wilder brother, I could get used to that.

Though I can't. Of course. Because I am not actually *attached* to a Wilder brother. Just…

Really, really kissing one.

My face goes red hot at the memory of all the kissing. And the feel of Clark's beard on the sensitive flesh of my inner thighs—and other places.

I take one more stab at keeping things simple. "I've got lots of work to do to make the wedding itself happen. I should be home addressing invite envelopes."

Lucy smiles at that, then turns to her friends. "What do you say we get together tomorrow night and knock off all the addressing over a bottle of wine? Then you'll have no excuse."

"Wine *after* addressing," I say, alarmed at the thought of red wine and pristine creamy invitations.

"Oh, right!" Lucy says. "Address, then wine, and we can finally start *Coffee Prince*."

"You guys watch Korean dramas?" That one's been around long enough that I've seen it on DVDs in Asian markets. If she'd named a more recent one, chances are I wouldn't have recognized it.

Rachel beams. "Yeah. My mom got me hooked."

I'm curious to know where K-dramas figure in Hanna's hierarchy of girliness. I raise an eyebrow in her direction, and she understands the unspoken question.

"I don't *hate* them," she says, with shrug. "And I can't convince these, uh, film buffs to watch the Marvel movies instead."

"I haven't watched any dramas," I admit. "People keep telling me I should. Or," I add, "assuming I do. But I don't, just because I haven't yet. But I'm down."

"Excellent," Rachel says. "Invitations, wine, and Gong Yoo."

Everyone gets a little dreamy-eyed over the Korean superstar actor.

"It's a plan," Amanda says. "So that means you can come to Vegas with us."

I'm about to restart my protests, when Lucy's phone vibrates against the tabletop. She reads the text, then holds it up triumphantly. It's a thread with Clark. My stomach twists with anticipation and dread in equal measures.

Her text:

We asked Jessa to come to Vegas with us. She's worried you want a guy's weekend and she'll be in the way. Thoughts? I won't tell her if you say "guy's weekend."

His:

I want her there. Tell her I said that.

26

JESSA

It's Wilder in Vegas, no joke. The Wilder brothers in Las Vegas are a sight to see. I mean, think about it. Five bearded mountain men, most at home in a tent or a hand-built shelter, leaves in their hair and beards, shooting or catching and skinning their own dinner, cooking over an open fire...

And the height of glitz, money, and fancy entertainment.

And the thing is? Every last one of them is capable of rising perfectly to the occasion.

You think the Wilder men are potent in quarter-zip base-layer polypro shirts? You should see them in suits.

I've lost every bet I've placed, and I'm going to blame it all on my total lack of concentration. I can't keep my eyes off Clark in the casino, to be honest. He looks as completely at ease here as he does in the woods, tossing dice down on a craps table, toying with whether to take another card, downing a drink, laughing with his brothers, and sliding me a flirtatious look across the table.

Those looks, by the way: Someone should package and

sell them. Maybe you could extract the pheromones straight out of them and bottle them—and then Rachel could peddle it to people who need a boost in their sex lives and make a fortune.

I'm trying to balance how much I want to tear his clothes off with some sense of self-preservation.

And basically, losing.

He pockets his chips and strolls away from the table—straight toward me. In the silvery-gray suit he's wearing—with a crisp white shirt and dark purple pocket square—his shoulders look even broader, his hips even narrower.

My inner thighs tighten in anticipation of Clark's touch and weight.

"Hey," he says.

"Looking good, Wilder," I tell him.

His smile blooms, slow and sexy.

Clark definitely got his beard trimmed professionally. Holy shit, those clean lines, and the tiny bit of white skin they reveal at the edge of his golden tan? I don't quite fan myself, but it's a close thing.

"Not so bad yourself, Olsen." His eyes take a leisurely trip from the spaghetti straps of my dress down over the long sheath. They spend a little extra time on my spiky heels. Noted.

"What's next?" I ask him.

"Blackjack, I think. What about you?"

I hold up my hands. "Blew through my budget for tonight. Can't seem to concentrate."

"Why's that?"

"Too many good looking Wilder men in suits."

He cocks his head. "Too many, huh?"

"One too many."

His gaze undresses me again, slow and knowing. "Distracted, huh?"

I nod.

He smirks. "Wanna come watch me play?"

"Sure."

I follow him to a blackjack table, where he's dealt in. He loses the first hand, then wins the second. He takes off his jacket and hangs it over the back of his chair, rolls his sleeves to the elbows. The crisp shirt blazes white against the golden tan of his gorgeous forearms. I'm glad I'm not trying to win anything. I'll just stand here and worship that long line of lean muscle, the one that ends in a thick bulge right below his elbow.

At the table next to us, Hanna and Easton are playing side by side. I can't hear what they're saying, but I can tell from their facial expressions and body language that they're giving each other the usual measure of shit. Easton says something to Hanna, and she dips her head, inclining it away from him, toward me. Hiding a smile.

A moment later, a beautiful woman in a long glittery blue gown takes the spot next to Easton's, and the next time I look up, Easton and the woman are chatting and laughing. Her hand finds his arm. Her shoulder bumps his. He bends to whisper something in her ear, and she laughs with delight, giving him doe eyes through her eyelashes. I flick my attention to Hanna, wondering what her reaction will be to the pageantry. Scorn, probably. I've gotten the feeling several times that she doesn't think much of Easton and his shenanigans—and even less of the women who fall for them.

But Hanna's gone from the table.

"Hey," she says from behind me. "I feel like shit. Too much sun and whiskey. I'm going to head back to the room. Didn't want to ditch you without warning. But you look like you're doing just fine." She ogles Clark's forearms, then rolls her eyes. "The Wilder brothers: God's gift to women, and they know it."

Huh.

Interesting. It's the only hint I've seen that Hanna isn't completely impervious to Wilder charms.

I turn my attention back to Clark. To his rumpled bedhead of red-brown waves and the crisper lines of his beard. The thick, straight lines of his eyebrows and his carved-from-marble cheekbones.

I can smell the faintest edge of an expensive aftershave, and I want to get close enough to trace it to its source with the tip of my nose and my lips. And beneath that, raw and musky, fresh sweat.

Holy crap, he smells good.

I'm leaning in to breathe his scent when he turns and catches me. The half-smile on his face disappears, replaced with something speculative. "Are you *smelling* me?" he murmurs.

My face flames.

"You *are.*" A smirk tips his lips.

The dealer hits Clark twice, at his request, and he turns over his face-down card to show 21. The dealer's expression doesn't change. Neither does Clark's, although I happen to know his winnings for the night now total over a thousand dollars.

"You're on a roll, huh?"

He shrugs. "Not too bad."

"Are you more of a play-while-you're-hot guy? Or a quit-while-you're-ahead?"

Another slow-blooming smile. One eyebrow tips up.

"I'm a quit-while-I'm-ahead..."

He pauses, the smile reaching its full, devasting potential.

"... and play-while-*you're*-hot guy."

My whole body goes tingly and liquid. Something in my face must betray me, because his smile drops away, and something dark and calculating comes into his expression. Tension bounces back and forth between us, multiplying in the thick atmosphere there.

"Your room or mine?" he murmurs.

IN THE ELEVATOR, after he cashes out, he crowds me against the wall, the gold-plated railing digging into my back. The moment spins out as we stand there—his eyes dark on my face, devouring me with his gaze. Then he cups my face with his big hands and ducks his head.

He moves slowly. So slowly, I register his bangs brushing my forehead, his breath gusting softly over my skin. The tingle of the chemistry between us, everywhere. Not just where his hands or breath touch my skin, but in every nerve ending, an all-over sparkle. He holds us like that for a long time, suspended in the anticipation. It feels so good, like waking up in the middle of the night on Christmas Eve, knowing what morning will bring.

Then his mouth lowers to mine. Soft. Slow. Kiss after kiss, each one a little deeper than the last, opening me up to him. Then just the tease of his tongue. A polite request. *May I?*

Hell yes.

Then not polite at all. I moan against the invasion of his tongue and the simultaneous press of his body—and his erection, thick under his suit pants—against me.

Public. We're in public. Cameras in the elevator. Casino security *everywhere*.

I don't care.

His tongue is absolutely wrecking me. And then, worse, he draws back for a moment and smiles at me.

Goodbye, legs.

He catches me as I start to slide down the wall.

That's when the bell pings and the doors slide open—it's only fourteen floors, and the elevator's fast. He picks me up, sweeping me off my feet and into the cradle of his arms. I gasp and laugh, and he's laughing too as he hurries me down the hall. He sets me down and works his keycard out of his pocket as I plunge my hands into his other pocket. He groans. Under the expensive wool of his suit, I stroke the thick, swollen head of his cock, working my thumb back and forth over the wet spot there while he struggles to get the keycard lined up with the card reader.

Then we're in, and he backs me against the door before it's even fully closed. His mouth is on mine and my dress is around my waist, his hand over the damp spot on my panties, between my legs, before the click comes.

His big, calloused hand cups the heat of my sex, and I can't help it, I rub myself shamelessly against it. The friction is good, too good. He sneaks his hand into my panties, eases a finger over my clit, and circles the bundle of nerves, swallowing my moan with a kiss.

He dips lower, finds me already wet for him, and groans.

"I want to be inside you," he says, his voice a rough whisper against my ear. "Do you want that?"

"Yes," I groan.

He sheds his jacket, rummaging in the inner pocket, pulling out a condom, tossing the jacket onto the floor. I unbutton his suit pants, slide a hand between the zipper and the swell of his cock before I unzip them, then work his boxer briefs free around his gorgeous erection, dropping pants and underwear to the floor.

He rolls the condom on, and pulls my panties down. "Step out." It's a command, in no uncertain terms, which starts a rising, tightening tension in my low belly.

I start to kick out of my shoes.

"Leave them," he growls.

I think I whimper. He grabs my ankle and untangles just one leg from my cream lace panties, leaving the shoe on. It's fucking hot, and I make a note to tell that to Clark, later, when the pulsing demand between my legs doesn't feel so much like a life-threatening emergency.

He plants one big hand against the heavy wooden door beside my head. Wraps the other tight around my waist and boosts me up enough so he can lower me onto his cock.

Oh. My. God.

"Jessa," he groans. "You feel so—"

Whatever he was about to say next turns into a grunt. Then, "So. Fucking. Good."

"You too." I'm breathless with it. He's big and hot and hard, and it's been a long time. He's stretching me, partly because he's big and I'm tight and partly because of the angle and the weight of my body against the base of his cock, and because he's strong enough to ruck his hips up against me and drive into me, even at this crazy angle. All those things are also putting pressure on my clit, rubbing it between his body and my pubic bone, and holy crap I'm climbing fast, so fast it's dizzying. "Don't stop," I instruct, and that makes him laugh, a rich, dark laugh that ends in a groan when I change the angle of my hips just slightly to get more of that rub.

I'm fevered. Desperate, and he can tell. "Does it feel good?" he demands.

All I can do is nod against him.

"I need your mouth," he says, and captures it with his. Then all I can do is hold on, lost in all the heat and wetness everywhere, his tongue and his cock and the rhythm of the kiss that matches the rhythm of his thrusts.

We go over together like that, kissing and fucking and clutching at each other, swallowing each other's groans and cries.

27

CLARK

She clears her throat.

I still have her pinned against the door. I slowly pull out, taking care with the condom, and lower her until her feet touch the floor again.

Cool air blows from somewhere across my bare, damp skin, and I feel, suddenly, regretful. Not about what we did. Only about how we did it. Like maybe I cheated her somehow. Rushed her. Kept her at arm's length by fucking her against a door instead of face-to-face on a mattress.

"Clark?" She sounds worried. She tugs her panties back on and her dress down, smoothing a hand over her front.

I frown. "I should have gotten us to the bed."

She smiles. Shakes her head. "I liked it that way." She tilts her head. "Didn't you?"

"Oh, yeah," I say, which makes her laugh, because it comes out so enthusiastically.

I take the condom into the bathroom, wrap it in a tissue, and dispose of it. I come back out, retrieve my pants from the floor, and hesitate before I toss them on the bed, digging in my suitcase for a pair of sweatpants. I start to unbutton my shirt.

"Let me."

Her fingers are nimble on my shirt buttons, and my cock, which should be completely down for the count, stirs. She tosses the shirt on top of my pants, leaving me in just my t-shirt, and her eyes stroke over the sight before her lips curve in a slight smile. A really fucking pretty smile. Then she turns her back to me, asking for an unzip. I lower the zipper slowly so I can savor the softness of her exposed back and the scent of her hair. The dress drops to the floor, leaving her in just bra and panties. She reaches for my shirt, slips into it, and buttons two buttons between her breasts.

She's still wearing her heels, and holy fuck, she looks hot in my shirt. I'm ready to get her out of it—already.

"I'm starving!" she says, before I can take a step toward her.

"Me too."

"I want Korean food." She kicks off her shoes now, and I'm only a little sad about it, because I also like the way her bare feet look, her toes wriggling in the pile of the hotel-room carpet.

"Sounds good to me."

I force myself to stop staring at her mile-long legs and the peekaboo of her panties between my shirt tails.

She grabs her phone and starts reading to me from a menu. I shake my head. "I put myself completely in your hands. I know bulgogi and bi bim bap and literally that's it. Oh, and Korean fried chicken. I've had that in Portland. You order, and I'll pick up the tab. Since I'm a big winner."

"Not fighting you on that. I lost a hundred dollars in twenty minutes." She rolls her eyes at herself.

"Yeah, but you bagged the big winner," I tease.

"I did, didn't I?" She gives me a self-satisfied smile that turns something over in my chest. "Fake dating is fun."

"I think it's the *real sex* you like," I tell her. "So how was your first post-marriage p-in-v? Did it live up?"

She bites her lip. "Um, the standard set by Reuben was not high. So it not only lived up, it blew my expectations away."

I try to pretend women say this kind of shit to me every day, but no dice. I'm grinning madly. She's grinning back. "Yeah." I want to be honest with her, because she was honest with me. "It was really fucking good, huh?"

She nods, her grin slowly fading as our gazes linger on each other.

Because it feels like the right thing to do, I lean over and kiss her. She kisses me back. Slow and tender. Something goes squishy in my chest, and I have to pull away. It's too much. Neither of us is grinning anymore.

She clears her throat and lifts her phone again, scrutinizing the Korean food menu.

Message received: It's too much for her, too.

And that's okay. That's why we've drawn all these lines around what we're doing. Why we put it in a "fake" box for so long. Why having an expiration date makes it doable.

Because this is the most either of us has to give right now.

I watch her face as her nose wrinkles and her mouth purses and her eyebrows draw together. So stinking cute.

She taps a bunch of times and hands me the phone with the delivery app open so I can enter my credit card info.

TWENTY MINUTES LATER, she unpacks a smorgasbord of Korean food onto the glass tabletop, explaining each dish as she adds it to the banquet. There's a soft tofu stew and a beef and vegetable stew, lots of steamed rice, two different kinds of fried chicken, and something that sounds a little like "kim pop," but that she says is usually written in the English alphabet as *gim bap*. It's seaweed wrapped around rice wrapped around radish and barbecued beef, but when I ask her if it's "Korean sushi," she tells me *no*, it's its own thing. "It's *gim bap*."

Whatever it is? I love it.

Also, Jessa is clearly in food heaven, and it's awesome to watch. She moans with pleasure when she tastes the soft tofu stew, and she stuffs the pieces of *gim bap* into her mouth and closes her eyes, which is distracting enough that I have to pause my eating and talk myself down.

The food is pretty damn amazing. I mean, it's not a shocker that I would like the double-fried fried chicken, or the fried chicken that's in the sweet-and-spicy *dakgangjeong* sauce. And I already knew I liked soju. The big surprise to me is kimchi. I wasn't expecting to like it, because the world is full of mean jokes about kimchi. But it's delicious. It's pickled cabbage, which, Jessa informs me, is mainly spicy when it's fresh, but the longer it ferments, the more sour it becomes. Everyone has a different opinion on when it's at its best—hence kimchi's complicated reputation.

While we eat, we chat about our time in Vegas so far. I tell her that last night, while she was at Cirque du Soleil's *O* with the women of the bridal party, I played wingman to Easton at a swanky bar in one of the other casino hotels. It took him three minutes to find his target, and another twenty-five minutes before they went upstairs together. Meanwhile, I sat at the bar and chatted with the bartender and the woman sitting next to me, who turned out to design and renovate RVs.

"Does she know the guy who's doing your renovations?" Jessa asks. I mentioned to her at some point that I've hired someone to redo the Airstream trailers I bought for the next phase of Wilder's Gilderness Glamping Experience.

"She said she'd heard of him—all good things—but that she's never met him. She was pretty interesting to talk to. She's itinerant. Lives out of her Airstream, travels the country redoing other people's."

"Was she cute?" she teases me.

I seriously consider the question. "Yes? Not my type, though."

"What's your type?"

You, I suddenly want to say. But I don't. I worry it'll come out too serious.

I shrug. "A little more down to earth than that. Not someone who lives out of an Airstream and roams the country."

"Even though you're a survival guru?"

"Yeah, sure, for days at a time. But I love my family and Rush Creek and the business. I'm more of a putting-down-roots guy. No coincidence that I was the first Wilder brother to get married."

She goes still. "Makes sense."

Damn it. I didn't mean to summon Emma back.

"Hey," she says slowly. "Do you think you could show me the survival stuff?"

"Like—what?"

"Like didn't you say you like to go into the woods with just a knife?"

"Yeah, but that's just me. I wouldn't subject you to that."

"Well, what about the beginner's version of that. I mean, not the Gilderness version, but, you know, just what a person absolutely needs to survive. Like those shiny blankets and iodine tablets and stuff."

I smile at her version of survival.

"Sure. Remind me when we get back and we'll plan something."

I snag a roasted potato with my chopsticks, then a pickled mushroom—two side dishes that came with our order. Both delicious.

"You're not bad with chopsticks," Jessa tells me, breaking the awkward silence.

I shrug. "When I was a kid, my parents made us use them when we ate at East Asian restaurants."

She tilts her head, a teasing grin lighting up her face. "Let's see what you're made of."

She challenges me to pick up increasingly small items with the chopsticks. I make it all the way down to a black bean, then fall apart over her single-grain-of-rice challenge. When I finally manage one, I feed it to her. Then another, because I really like the way her soft lips close around the chopsticks. Then I set down the chopsticks and roll my chair close to her and kiss her. She tastes tangy and spicy and I can't get enough. I brace myself over her, kissing her harder, licking into her mouth. She reaches up and clutches my head, pulling me down. The chair starts to roll, and I chase her, both of us laughing and kissing and gasping for breath in between. I drop to my knees, eyes locked on the gap between my shirt tails, the triangle of cream lace between her soft thighs.

The door lock beeps.

"Shit. Kane."

I lunge to my feet, and Jessa yanks the tails of my shirt together and starts trying to fasten the remaining buttons.

I'd completely forgotten about him. I'd had a vague intention of texting him and telling him to go crash with Easton (assuming Easton's room was not also occupied, which maybe was a long shot?), but somewhere between the mind-melting sex and the fucking awesome Korean food, I'd lost all track of that idea.

He steps into the room, and it only takes one look at the expression on his face before I realize that my evening is over.

28

CLARK

"What happened to you?" I demand.

"I did something—"

Kane stops, registering for the first time that Jessa's here, too—and naked except for my shirt. He shoots me an apologetic look. "Hey. I didn't mean to interrupt."

"Don't be ridiculous," Jessa says briskly. "It's your room!" She looks from him to me and back again. "And don't go all bro-code on me. Clark and I can be together any time we want at home."

She grabs her dress and shoes and ducks into the bathroom. I want to beg her not to change, to tell her how much I like her just like this, relaxed and wearing my shirt—but the gutted look on Kane's face stops me.

When she comes out again, she's back to the way she started the evening: dress and shoes and hair restored to some semblance of order.

She starts bustling around, consolidating food, cleaning

up, and making a plate for Kane which she hands to him. He looks at it like he's not even seeing it, sets it on the table, and sinks onto the bed like his legs aren't strong enough to hold him up.

"I'd, um, better head back to my room," Jessa says, taking a good long look at him, then at me. "Hanna's not feeling well, and I should check on her."

Kane shoots her a grateful look, and she gives him a warm smile.

She gives me a quick, soft open-mouthed kiss, then vanishes out the door.

We both watch her go. When I turn back to Kane, he winces. "I'm sorry I chased her away."

"It's fine. She understands."

"Looks like you guys—like things are good?"

I nod, because if I try to start explaining about fake and real, the conversation will be about me, and it's pretty damn clear Kane needs it to be about him.

"She's nice. She seems like she's good for you."

It feels like the biggest understatement of my life, but I can't get into that with him right now. "You okay?" I ask him, instead.

He paces a few steps away from me. Goes to the window, pushes back the curtains, looks down at the Strip, bright and unreal below us. "What if I said I don't know?"

I raise my eyebrows at him. "I'd worry. You're not a drama queen, dude, so if you're shook up, that's not good. What the hell just happened?"

"I just—" He shakes his head. His eyes are a little wild. "I hooked up with a woman I've never met before in my life and had sex with her in the hotel family bathroom and I don't know her name."

"Jesus," I say, startled, because of all the things I expected my boy-next-door brother to say, it wasn't that.

"I was out with Gabe and Brody. We were all drinking. And I was telling them it had been a while since I'd gotten any..."

I shake my head, knowing where this was going.

"They were all, you have to break the drought, bro, you have to get back on the horse. I said, I'm not like you guys, I don't just pick up women in bars. And Brody was like, 'That's because you're trying too hard to be a good guy. Pretend you're an asshole. Be a guy who has one night stands all the time. Be Easton.'"

"Does that shit *work*?" I demand. "Like, I'm not a doctor but I play one on TV, and I can deliver your baby?"

Kane manages a laugh, but he still looks pale. "It works," he affirms. "It fucking works. Or at least it worked this time. I sat down next to her and said, 'Can I buy you a drink?' and she said yes, and we started chatting. About nothing, you know. Like, she was asking why I was in town, and I told her, and she said every guy she'd met this week was in town for a bachelor party, and I said, that probably meant she'd been hit on by every guy she'd met because she was beautiful, and she —" His eyes get big. "She looked surprised. Startled. She said, no, it wasn't like that, she wasn't the kind of woman who got hit on all the time or anything, and I asked if that meant she felt like she was due? If she'd be game to be hit on tonight."

"Nice," I say admiringly, because Kane's apparently got game.

"I was channeling Easton, I swear," he says. "I kept thinking, 'WWED—what would Easton do?' and then it just came out of my mouth, this alpha, charming, shit. And the next thing I know—" He waves his hands helplessly.

"How do you get from sitting at the bar and flirting to sex in a bathroom?"

Because let's face it, that's the question anyone would have in this situation, right?

"God, Clark," he says. "I'm such a fucking cliché. She looks up at me with these big, long-lashed eyes. I'm sitting there feeling like the biggest man on campus, which isn't even a thing I ever wanted to be. But this girl makes me feel like it, and I can't resist. I can't even believe she doesn't get hit on 24/7. And she says, 'I'm going to the bathroom. Family bathroom. There's a couch in there.'"

My mouth falls open.

"It was like an out of body experience. I'm getting up from the bar, I'm walking to the bathroom, I'm trying the handle. In a dream fog. It's unlocked. I'm pushing it open, and she's standing there, just waiting for me, with her shirt in her hands, and her perfect little tits—"

I cut him off. "Got it."

Kane turns dazed eyes to me. The wrecked look on his face is starting to make more sense.

"I didn't use a condom," he says. "She said she was clean and had an IUD, and I believed her. I don't know what the fuck got into me. I just—I think I just wanted it. To be someone else for a night."

"We all do sometimes," I say, the "amen" in my voice.

"But what was I thinking? Fucking a stranger without protection?"

"Look. You're not the first guy ever to lose his head. You'll get yourself tested. And as for the rest—if she says she has an IUD, she probably does. Who lies about that shit?"

"I mean, people do," he says.

We both sit on that for a moment.

"Does she know how to reach you?"

He shakes his head. "I made it as far as the street, and then I ran back in. I was like, I need to at least know how to get in touch with her, right? Or give her a way to get in touch with me. But she was gone. I couldn't find her anywhere. And no one else had seen her. It really was like I'd fucking dreamed her."

"Then there's not a hell of a lot you can do, is there?"

"No."

"So stop beating yourself up, Kane. It doesn't accomplish anything, and it hurts."

There's a strange faraway look in his eyes.

"Seriously. Quit it. Look at you. You're a fucking mess. You can't keep shitting on yourself about it."

"No," he says. "It's not that."

"It's not what?"

He's lost me. I stare at him, waiting for some explanation.

"That's not why I'm a mess," he says. "I mean, yeah, I feel like a total schmuck. I should have at least swapped numbers with her. Or made her tell me her name. And yeah, it's a fucking asshole move to do what I did without using a condom, no matter what she said about it being okay, and no matter that I just got tested. But that's only half of it."

"What's the other half?" I ask cautiously, because if that's only half of it? I'm not sure I want to know the other half.

Kane takes a deep breath, like he's gathering himself. For

a moment, his gaze gets even further away, like he's seeing back an hour ago. Like he's still there in the bathroom with her. Then he blows out the breath, nods his head, and says:

"It was the best sex I've ever had."

29

JESSA

On the last night in Vegas, Amanda, Hanna, Rachel, Lucy and I gather in Lucy's room for a girls' night. We binge on snack food that Amanda picked up earlier and pour ourselves hotel room glasses full of cheap red wine, courtesy of a trip Rachel and I made to the liquor store.

We settle under the hotel's extra blankets and watch a few more episodes of *Coffee Prince*, streaming on Amanda's computer.

"Hey, Han," Amanda says. "You okay? Never seen you cry over a show—"

"Nope," says Hanna. "Nope, nope, nope, not crying."

None of us try to argue with her, even though there are wet streaks down her cheeks. Amanda passes her a box of tissues, and Hanna glares at her, then yanks several from the box and mops her face.

"I just—" she says, sniffling. "I like how he accepts her either way. Girl or boy, what she is doesn't matter to him. It's the person inside."

Rachel reaches out a hand and rests it on Hanna's arm, and, surprisingly, Hanna doesn't pull away.

"I was thinking..." Hanna begins, then stops. She starts again. "I've been thinking about trying dating again. Maybe with Tinder."

Every eyebrow in the room shoots ceilingward.

"Dating and I don't go well together," she explains to me.

"But Tinder?" Lucy asks.

Hanna aims a glare at her. "What are my alternatives?" she demands. "All the rest of you think moving to a small town and falling for a mountain man is a viable life plan. I already fucking *live* in a small town, and I wouldn't bang a Wilder if you paid me."

"None of them?" Amanda asks innocently.

"None of them," Hanna growls.

"Legit choice," Lucy tells her. "It's down to Kane and Easton, anyway, which means it's down to Kane."

I don't quibble with this assessment, although I know I should. No matter how I feel about Clark, he's not mine to have. He's not ready to be taken. And I'm leaving. But I can't make myself say any of that out loud.

There's a hefty part of me that doesn't want Clark to be an available Wilder. For Hanna or anyone else.

"And Kane's my business partner," Hanna says, "so even if I weren't fundamentally opposed to the very idea of banging a Wilder, it's not gonna happen." She sighs. "If I wanted to date women, I'd probably be all set, but I'm not most straight guys' idea of their fantasy woman."

"You can change their minds," Rachel says gently. "Eun Chan changed Han-kyul's mind."

Hanna looks like she's about to respond, but she falls

silent. We all do, sneaking looks at her, but the tears are gone and her face is blank, locked back into Hanna neutral. Still, now I know that no matter how tough she comes off, she's vulnerable like any of us.

Rachel breaks the silence. "Hey, gals. I did a party for a Vegas-based friend last night, and I have giveaway freebie merch left over. I thought I could give it to you all as party favors for the Vegas trip."

"I never turn down free sex merch," I say, making everyone else laugh.

"We knew we liked you," Hanna says.

I have to admit, those words from Hanna of all people give me the fuzzies.

Rachel brings out tubes of warming gel, nubby clit-stimulating finger caps, and small bullet vibes. "I'm warning you," she says, waving the bright-colored lipstick-sized cases. "Most women can't get off to these things. Not strong enough vibrations. But they're still fun. And you could use 'em on your nipples and get something more powerful between your legs."

That instantly brings to mind an image of Clark pounding into me.

We haven't been alone together since last night, before Kane interrupted. All day today we were surrounded by Wilders, significant others, and friends, as we rushed from appointments to shows to meals. Clark did sit next to me at lunch and hold my hand under the table, which was so delicious that I could barely taste my food, but other than that, the best we could do was sneak secret smiles. Not only does Clark actually smile, but he has a whole repertoire: shy, smirky, happy. They pretty much all make me want to grab him by his tie and yank him upstairs.

"Jessa," Amanda says in a coy voice that reeks of trouble—and also proves that she mind-reads. "How are things with you and Clark?"

"Beware!" Hanna says, bouncing on the bed. "She is grooming you for sister-in-law. She wants more cousins for her children. And now that she and Heath are fucking again, there may be more Kenning children!"

"We're not 'fucking,'" Amanda says primly. "We're 'making love.'"

Hanna scowls at her. "Rumor has it you were *fucking* all over the mountain at the Tinsel and Tatas Games and Gala."

"Rumor is very uncouth." But Amanda bites back a smile.

Rachel tilts her head and fills me in: "Amanda and Heath were in a brutal dry spell that appears to now be—"

"Wet," Hanna finishes.

We all wince at the unwanted visual, Amanda most of all.

And, unfortunately, the topic of Amanda's (past) marital woes has not caused her to lose her train of thought. "So?" she demands of me. "How are things between you and my brother?"

What *is* that expression on her face?

Oh. She's laughing at me.

And I realize:

She has still not completely bought the fiction.

She knows—or at least she strongly suspects—that we're up to something.

I really don't think anything *ever* gets past Amanda.

Now, it occurs to me, would be an excellent time to fess up.

It would be the perfect time to tell my new friends that Clark and I are fake boyfriend and girlfriend, even though we are real fuck buddies. It would be the perfect time to ask their forgiveness for deceiving them.

I open my mouth to tell the the truth.

But nothing comes out.

I think it's because I don't know what the truth is anymore.

All I manage is, "Things are really good."

It feels true, which makes my chest hurt a little.

Amanda gives me a long, sharp look.

Even if I wanted to give her a more nuanced description of reality, I can't. The choice to tell Amanda the truth is Clark's, not mine. So I counter her sharp look with my best innocent one.

She narrows her eyes some more; I widen mine.

Rachel looks from one of us to the other and back again and says, "Hmm."

"Well, good," Hanna says, apparently oblivious to all these dynamics. "Because Amanda told us Reuben the Fuckhead cheated on you with Whatserface and they were both on that Gilderness trip, so you deserve something good, and there's nothing good-er than Clark."

"Better," Rachel corrects, apparently automatically. She was a librarian before she started training to be a sex therapist.

"I mean, yeah," Hanna says. "But I kind of mean good-er, too."

I know exactly what she means.

"I've read the book," Rachel tells me quietly.

"Reuben's book?"

"Yeah."

I duck my head.

"You have *nothing* to be ashamed of," Rachel says fiercely. "That is such a dick move! Pre-justifying his assholery to his public!"

I hadn't actually thought about it that way, but yeah! On top of everything else, he made a pre-emptive strike against me in the court of public opinion. I hadn't needed any reason to hate Reuben even more, but now I have one.

"He better stay away from the Wilders," Lucy says, growly.

"I love you guys." It just pops out.

They all swivel to me, various shades of surprised, and for a long moment I think, *Whoops*.

Then Rachel grins and says, "We love you, too, babe."

30

JESSA

I'm back from Vegas less than a week when Edelweiss's owner, Lew Raglan, wakes me Saturday morning with a phone call.

I don't even have to answer it to know that it should come with the "calls that suck" ringtone. It's never good news when a wedding venue calls you at 8 a.m. on a Saturday morning.

"There was a fire," he says glumly.

I grip the phone tighter. "Is everyone okay?"

"Yeah, thankfully. No one was near it. It was an electrical fire." He takes a deep breath. "We're doing everything we can to get the repairs done by Lucy and Gabe's date, but unfortunately, it's going to be super tight. If you want to find another venue, we'll refund your deposit."

He sounds wretched, and I think of all the phone calls like this one he has to make today. I know Edelweiss's business is strong enough to rebound from this, but it's not going to be fun.

"I'm so sorry about the fire, Lew," I say. "Thank you for

giving us that option. I'll talk to the couple and see what they want to do."

We hang up, and I roll out of bed, dashing off a text to Lucy that I need to chat with her about wedding logistics.

We're about to have brunch! She texts back. *Come join us!*

We who? I want to text, but don't. Still, every fiber of my being hopes "we" includes Clark. He's been on a trip most of this week, off the grid and out of texting range.

I did get one, though: *What happened in Vegas? Wouldn't mind if it happened again.* 🌵

I sat and grinned stupidly at it for waaay too long.

I text Lucy back, *Thanks—can I bring anything?* And she texts back, *Your badass self.*

Turns out "we" includes just about the whole Wilder crew, including Clark, freshly showered and giving off the bright, delectable scent of soap in a five-foot radius.

"Hey," he says, giving me a lopsided smile.

"Hey yourself."

He holds his arms open, and I walk into them. There's something about that—just a hug—that feels realer than anything else. You hug someone you like.

Also, Clark gives amazing hugs. Big, warm, solid, arms-around-you hugs. Like real-live teddy bear good.

Except when he draws me closer so his abs brush my belly. And molten heat washes down to my thighs. That's not so teddy bear. Nngh.

I pull back before we stop being family friendly.

He dips his head and whispers, "Later," like he knows.

Brunch is insane—a huge waffle bar with every topping you can imagine, Barb and Geneva pumping waffles out of three different irons and handing them out to Wilders, who load them up with chocolate and caramel sauce, maple and fruit syrup, strawberries, raspberries, applesauce, cinnamon, and whipped cream.

I could get used to doing things the Wilder way.

After brunch, I head to the kitchen and talk to Lucy, who takes the news of the fire like a champ, but says she definitely wants to check out the venues that still have availability. "I just know how stressed I'd be crossing my fingers that they'll be up and running in time."

I tell her I totally support her decision, and as soon as we're sure all the dishes and pans are put away, I whip out my phone and book a bunch of venue visits. Unfortunately, the venue decision (once again) has to be made in a hurry, which means visits today and tomorrow. Amanda's photographer also canceled on us this week, because her pet snake is having surgery the week of the wedding.

Yeah, I crossed her permanently off the list, even though her work is solid. We were already tapping bottom when we chose her. My two favorite photographers were booked up by the time Lucy and Gabe got engaged. Another woman whose work I admire isn't working this fall because she's having a baby.

So now I'm going to have to take the photography appointments we booked for this weekend, and probably make a photography judgment call for the couple. I find Lucy —in the kitchen showing Amanda's oldest how to dispose of bacon grease in a can—and break this news to her.

"You can decide for us," she says. "I trust you."

"That's a lot of responsibility." I laugh. "The photos are the one thing that endures forever. You sure about that?"

"I'll go with you," Clark says. "Then you can blame me if

the photos suck."

I hadn't even realized he was standing in the door. Filling the doorway, one hand up on the frame, his head almost to the sill. In just a short time his beard has lost that just-trimmed look, and I can't decide which I like more—Clark-in-a-suit with beard trimmed, or the Viking in the doorway, in his t-shirt, *No fire, no water, no shelter. Change one of these and you have HOPE.*

Lucy looks from him to me and back and smiles.

So that's how the Viking and I end up sitting side by side across from Jane Early as she shows us her really, really bad wedding photography portfolio.

She's not the first, either. We have already seen some truly atrocious portfolios this morning. After each visit, we recap the horrors in Clark's truck, finally letting ourselves laugh—at the photographer who used soft focus every time and the one who managed cleavage shots of every woman he photographed—including one disturbing multigenerational shot down the dresses of great-grandma, grandma, mom, and bride.

"Great-grandma nip!" I howled in the car. "I will never unsee that!"

"But it wasn't as bad as the photoshopping early this morning, that one of the groom putting the ring on the bride? They obviously came from two separate photos, and the angles were all off. And the line of her nose was ragged."

"Painful," I agreed.

Jane Early is not that bad. Not *quite*.

"I like to get candids," she says. "I like to capture all the moods of the couple."

Which is probably why in the set she's showing us, the

bride looks like she's about to kill the groom. Or burst into tears. Or lean over and lose the contents of her stomach.

"Interesting approach," Clark says. He shoots me a look that almost makes me burst out laughing. I stuff it down, though.

We make it back to the truck without howling.

"Jesus," he says. "Those were some slim pickins."

I don't try to deny it.

He frowns. "I want to show you something. Will you humor me?"

"Of course."

We drive to an apartment complex in town, and Clark rings the buzzer. Kane's voice comes through the intercom, and he buzzes us up. He's standing in the doorway when we crest the stairs. "What's this about?" he asks Clark.

"Just let us in," Clark says.

Kane shrugs, steps back, lets us into the apartment, and I instantly understand. The walls are covered with photographs, beautiful, pro-quality framed photographs. Most of them are candids of his family as well as other people, but plenty of them are landscapes, too—some of the most beautiful pictures I've ever seen of Rush Creek.

"Wow," I say. I recognize some of the photos that appeared on Clark's walls, including several of Emma. She was very beautiful, damn it.

Kane gives an eloquent Wilder one-shoulder shrug.

"No," I say. "Don't downplay it. You're really talented."

"It's just a hobby." Another shrug.

"Maybe it shouldn't be?" I touch my finger to my lips. "How would you feel about shooting your brother's wedding?"

He ducks his head. "I wouldn't have any idea how to do that."

I look at the photos on his wall again. "I think you would. But you don't have to do it like a professional photographer. Just do it like yourself. It would make me feel a hell of a lot better about hiring the least awful photographer we saw today if I knew you were shooting, too."

"Isn't that a conflict?" Clark asks.

"Totally reasonable question; wedding photographers can get super testy about that stuff, or even have clauses in their contracts. But Michael Rich"—AKA the least awful photographer we saw today—"is a pretty mellow guy and won't give a shit."

Kane shrugs again. "Sure," he says. "I'll give it a shot."

We thank him and clear out, heading back to Clark's truck. As we're pulling out, a call comes in from Lucy.

"We're sticking with Edelweiss," she says. "Lew can guarantee that if the renos aren't done, they can do the wedding outdoors, under a tent—and you know what the mountain views are like. Plus, I just can't give up the on-premise hot-springs thing."

"I don't blame you." I have a quick mental flash back to the sight of Clark, glistening and steaming in the Edelweiss springs.

"Gabe wants to make dinner for you and Clark to thank you for doing the photography appointments today. That was above and beyond."

I turn to Clark. "Gabe wants to make us dinner."

"Never turn down free food," he says. "Even if one of my brothers cooked it."

"I heard that!" Gabe says. "I'm on speaker!"

"I know you are, dope," Clark says affectionately. "So am I."

AFTER DINNER AT GABE'S, we go back to Clark's apartment and have crazy monkey sex all over everything.

I'm exaggerating, but really just a little. It's like the Vegas thing, times ten, except that this time he drops to his knees in his front hall and makes me come with his mouth before we make our way through the house, de-flowering all the surfaces. It's frantic and hot and super sexy, and by the time we're done, I've come two more times, once against the rub and roll of his pubic bone, and once against his thumb pressed to my clit.

Then we drape ourselves on his couch and watch the newest M. Night Shyamalan movie, which isn't bad because I have to bury myself in his shoulder and chest, clutching him like a schoolgirl.

At the end of the day, he drives me home, and when I get ready to climb down from his truck, he says, "I had a good time with you today."

"Me too," I say.

"I haven't laughed that much in a long time."

"Me neither."

He leans across the gap between us, takes my chin in his hand, and draws me in for a kiss.

I climb down, thinking if I had to choose between making Clark laugh and making him come, I'd choose laughter every time.

31

CLARK

Jessa sticks a finger into the bundle of fabric I'm attempting to tie around a small brown box full of wedding favors.

"Under, over," she says, showing me where I've fucked up the knot for the tenth time. "Aren't knots like a big thing for wilderness survival?"

"Knots like the kind that let you climb trees and rocks, not knots like the kind that look beautiful on wedding favors."

She wraps her arms around me from behind, her small curves soft against my shoulder blades as she attempts to straighten me out. Mmmph. And hell, yes. Long may this demo continue.

I've asked to see her a couple of times since the day we spent interviewing photographers (and the night we spent defiling my apartment), but she's been busy with a couple of big weddings—including the Wilder one—and I've had trips, and we haven't been able to work around each other's schedules.

Seeing her this afternoon is like getting to draw a full breath for the first time in days.

And it's pure bliss to have her arms around me and her hands over mine, even if it's to make small fabric-covered knotted favor boxes.

All Wilder brothers plus Lucy, Amanda, Rachel, Hanna, my mom and Geneva, Lucy's mom and Gregg, Amanda's husband Heath, and Amanda's two older kids, Anna and Noah, are gathered to tie the boxes. Kane asked to be exempted, on the grounds that he is already the backup photographer, and Easton asked to be exempted, on the grounds that he is obviously never intending to get married and thus will never be able to call in a return favor.

Lucy shot them down, both of them.

I didn't bother trying. Partially because I knew I'd get shot down too, but I have to admit it, mostly because I wanted to see Jessa.

She looks particularly hot today, in a tight-fitting pink t-shirt and short shorts. I've had trouble keeping my eyes off her.

Even when I succeed in not ogling her, I'm hyper aware of where she is—bantering with my sister and the other women, chatting with my mom and Geneva, asking Anna questions about her softball summer camp.

With the fifteen of us collaborating, we make short work of the boxes, then clean up all the fabric scraps and bits of thread that have glued themselves to our clothes, the rug, and the chairs.

"I have an announcement," my mother says.

"How do you feel about announcements?" Amanda stage whispers to Hanna. "Are they like confessions?"

"Sort of," Hanna replies.

I have no idea what they're talking about.

"I mean, this is sort of a confession," my mother says. "Depending on how you define announcement versus confession."

"I can hack it," Hanna says generously. "This isn't a girls' night, so the rules are different."

"It's sort of like a girls' night." Easton scowls, but I know he's full of shit. He was enjoying tying the boxes earlier.

We all turn to my mother, who looks like she's going to be sick. She opens her mouth, closes it, then opens it again and says, "Geneva and I are... together."

There's a small moment of silence, then a rush of approving noises.

"Cool!" Amanda says. "I like Geneva."

Geneva blushes.

"I knew it!" Noah says triumphantly.

I give him a quelling look.

"You said she was your friend," Noah explains to my mom, unquelled. "Which Clark says means she's actually your girlfriend."

"What I said was a little more complicated than that. But hey, Geneva, welcome to the Wilder wackiness." I reach across the table and shake her hand. Then I get up, go to my mom's side, and cover her hand with both of mine.

My mother shoots me a quick, grateful look. There are tears in her eyes.

"Amen," says Rachel. "Dating a Wilder: Not for the faint of heart." But the look she gives Brody is brimming with love, and the look he gives her back makes my chest hurt.

It's really fucking good to see my family happy. And I realize, maybe this is the first time in a really long time that I've truly felt that way. That their happiness is my happiness, and not just a thing that sits alongside my sadness.

My mother is clearly puzzled. "Isn't anyone shocked? Or—don't you have questions for me? Or—maybe someone is going to need therapy?"

"I already need therapy," Amanda says, shrugging. Hanna frowns in her direction, and Amanda rolls her eyes.

"I have a question," Anna says.

We brace ourselves, because tweens can say absolutely anything.

"Is it, like a friends-to-lovers kind of thing?"

Ah, eleven.

"Yes," my mother says, giving Geneva a loving look. "It is like that kind of thing."

"Makes sense," Anna says sagely.

We all exhale.

"I'm shocked," Gabe admits, "but let's face it, I'm usually shocked by stuff that I should see coming."

"So fucking true," Brody tells him, and Gabe flashes him a quick middle finger.

"And it's like, good shocked," Gabe adds quickly. "Amanda's right. Geneva is cool."

My mother has tears running down her face now.

"You guys," she says.

I couldn't have put it better myself.

"Clark."

Jessa and I are headed out from the DIY party when my mom stops me on the front steps of Gabe's house.

Jessa takes a few steps away, giving us a little privacy.

My mom puts a hand on my arm. "Thank you."

I smile at my mom. "For what?"

"For holding my hand and being supportive."

I raise my eyebrows. "What did you think I'd do?"

"I wondered. You all loved your dad an awful lot." Her green eyes search my face, worried.

"But none of us wanted you to be lonely forever."

She gives me a long, considering look.

And for the first time, I get it. "Oh," I say, and she nods.

All this time, my mother and I have had parallel griefs. How could I have missed that?

I rub my forehead. "I guess I thought he died so long ago that you weren't still grieving and lonely. Or maybe kids are just selfish and can't really think about their parents' pain."

She smiles at that. "I'm sure that's part of it. And I wouldn't have wanted you to think about it too much. As to the other point—we had six children and eighteen years together. It has taken me a long time to want to start again. And I had to find the right person." Her expression goes dreamy. "Finding the right person is key." She slides an arm around my back. "I'm glad you found Jessa. You don't know how much good it does my mama heart to see you so happy."

My first impulse is to dismiss what she's saying—not out loud, but in my head. *It's not real.*

But then I look over at Jessa. She's standing a small distance away, fiddling with her phone, swiping with her long, slim fingers. Her hair is swept back over her shoulders, and there's a little wrinkle in the middle of her forehead that I know means she's trying to solve something related to work. Her top teeth are worrying her lower lip, and, yeah, I want to be the only one biting that lip, but mostly? I want to know what's in her head.

That's real.

"Clark?" my mother asks, reaching up to touch my face.

The kisses are real.

The touching is real.

The sex is real. (Oh, hell, *yes*, it is.)

The fun we have together is real.

I take a deep breath.

"Yeah," I say. "I'm really happy."

32

JESSA

"Your place or mine?" Clark asks, as I belt myself into the passenger seat of his truck.

He's joking/not joking, because when I look up at him, his eyes tell me what he wants to do to me as soon as possible, and I don't feel like arguing with those eyes.

"Doesn't matter," I say.

"I like your place."

I like that you like my place.

I'm feeling all the things. Full of everything. How beautiful Lucy's wedding is going to be, with those adorable, knotted boxes and Edelweiss and the band I hired three days ago and Kane's photos (no matter how shitty a job Michael Rich does). The feel of putting my arms around Clark's big body and guiding his ridiculously gorgeous, calloused man hands through that funny knot.

Being part of that moment when Barb Wilder let her kids know who Geneva really is to her.

And the tender moment afterwards, too, Barb full of gratitude and love for Clark, and then:

Yeah. I'm really happy.

Clark's words to his mom.

I want to believe them.

I want so much to believe them.

When we get to my place, we don't talk about it, we just go upstairs.

He doesn't fall on me just inside the door this time. He waits until we're standing in the living room, and then he slowly draws me close and kisses me tenderly. My heart thuds, blood rushing through all my veins, heating for him. We kiss for a long time, and then he strips me out of my clothes, leaving them in a pile on the living room floor, and I do the same to him.

I take his hand and lead him down the hall into my bedroom, and we kiss some more. His bare skin is hot against mine, and all the textures are just right—smooth in places and soft as satin, rough in other places. And he's hard as a wall under the softness. I had forgotten how perfect skin against skin feels, how right.

I could stay like this for hours and hours, and it starts to feel like that, like time's stretched out and the kisses blend into each other, until I can't imagine taking my mouth away from his. I want him to lift me up and slowly lower me to the bed, never stopping the kiss. I want him to slide into me while his mouth still covers my mouth, while his tongue is still strong and slick against mine.

Instead, he turns me around so my back leans against his front. His heat is at my back, his cock hard at the base of my spine. He kisses my neck, my shoulders, my shoulder blades, down my back to the dimples of my ass, and then he bends me gently over the bed and parts me from behind. He finds my core—wet silk—and slides his fingers in, testing, working me, his mouth still on my back.

It feels so good, my legs go limp.

He presses into me, slowly. Just a tiny bit at a time, filling and spreading me so slowly that my body begs silently for more, his mouth hot on my neck, his hands wrapped around to find my nipples, which he tweaks and teases.

It feels so fucking good.

But I wish I could see his face.

So I knew for sure. If it was real.

One hand slips down and cups me. His fingers slide between the lips of my sex and find the swollen bundle of nerves at the top. One hand on my breast, the other on my clit, he drives me up, up, up.

I feel so full with him inside me from behind like this. So full, so stretched. He's deep, but gentle, a long, sweet, liquid silver stroke. I arch my back and change the angle for him, and he groans my name, his fingers speeding on my body.

With his lips on my neck and his fingers circling my clit and his other hand lightly tugging my nipple, I come so hard on his cock that I make him come, too, and he cries out—my name—and sinks down over me, the two of us bent over the bed.

So, so good.

In that moment, full of him, covered by him, I don't have to see his face to know it's real.

33

CLARK

I wake up slowly, with a rush of warmth and memory.

Jessa.

My arms full of her. The sensation of filling her. A fullness in my chest I couldn't breathe around.

I put a hand out, reaching for her.

The bed's empty.

My stomach lurches.

The first year after Emma died, waking up was awful. The fear and grief came first, with a sensation like plunging off a cliff, before I was fully awake. I only knew I was alone and that something important was lost.

Sometimes it was worse when I remembered what it was.

Sometimes was better, because I could look back at the past months and know that even though the grief was deep and awful, it wasn't as deep or as awful or as constant as it used to be. I could tell myself that things would get better.

I haven't woken up with those same feelings for a long time.

But now the cool sheet under my hand brings a similar sensation, a jolt of fear, a lurch in my gut.

I pat the bed all over, like I might have misplaced Jessa somewhere under the covers.

Sitting up, I swing my legs over the side of the bed. "Jessa?" I call, tentatively.

There's a groan from the other room, and it brings me to my feet, heart pounding. I rush into the living room, and she's doubled over on the couch. She looks up at me, face pale, skin drawn. "Ugh," she says. "Stomach flu."

In my head, Emma presses a hand to her chest. *Something's wrong, Clark.*

It's okay, baby, go back to sleep.

I'm already on the move, racing back to the bedroom, grabbing for my sweatpants and t-shirt, raggedly thrusting a leg in, almost falling over in my haste. My own stomach cramps, but I ignore it.

"We're going to the emergency room."

Jessa groans and crawls into one corner of the couch, pressing her face into the pillow.

"Jessa, come on."

"No," she mumbles into the pillow. "I'll be fine. It's just stomach flu."

I grab her, sit her up. She looks at me, dazed. The color of her face makes my chest ache.

"We need to go now, Jessa. Come on."

My chest is so tight I can barely breathe, and my heart is racing. She's real. This is real. Everything I feel for her is real, and so is my fear, so real I can barely keep it from drowning me.

"Clark, I'm fine," she says. Her voice is a little stronger

now, and the dazed look has gone out of her eyes, her brows drawn together in confusion and concern.

"Now!" My voice is sharp. I grab her sweatshirt, draped over the arm of the couch. "Put that on."

"Clark, you're being ridiculous. I'm *fine.*"

I start trying to get her into the sweatshirt, but she pulls away. "Clark, stop it!" Her voice is tight.

"We're going."

She shoves at my shoulder. "I'm not a child! You don't get to tell me what to do!"

Her voice is raised now, to match the fever in mine. We're going to wake the late-sleeping neighbors if we keep it up, but I don't care. You don't make the same mistake twice, not when the stakes are so high. My stomach cramps again, worse.

I scoop her up from the couch and carry her towards the door. She struggles in my arms.

"Are you out of your mind?" she demands. "Put me down!" She pushes hard against my chest, sending me off balance. I careen into the wall, and a wave of dizziness washes over me.

Wrenching herself out of my arms, she stumbles to her feet and stares at me.

I don't know what she sees there, but her face softens. "Clark," she says gently. Then she shuts up, goes pale, and closes her eyes.

My own stomach cramps. Hard, and a surge of nausea descends, so fierce it blacks my vision.

"Shit, shit, shit," I say.

I run to the bathroom and empty the contents of my stomach.

When I come back to earth, there's a hand in my hair and

one on my shoulder, and then there are arms around me, pulling me upright.

I swipe an arm across my mouth and wait for my vision to clear. It does, slowly. While Jessa watches, quietly, considering, I rinse my mouth at the sink. Jessa's hand strokes slowly down my back. I raise my head and meet her eyes in the mirror. She's faintly green and drawn, but one corner of her mouth is lifted.

"I told you it was stomach flu," she says wryly. "Did you get the really bad cramps first?"

I nod.

"I bet it's norovirus. Fast moving and awful. One time half a wedding party came down with that. You can imagine. It was disastrous."

She's wearing one of my t-shirts and nothing else. Pretty sure I was going to take her to the hospital dressed just like that. Without thinking twice about it.

I can't smile, because the line between alive and gone is so thin. It's so easy to be wrong. It's so easy to lose someone. And she is so fucking beautiful and funny and—even white and wincing with pain—sexy.

We limp back out to the living room. She tiptoes into the kitchen, finds a ginger ale and makes me sip it.

"Clark," she says quietly. "Clark. Sit down."

I do. The ginger ale tastes good, but my stomach cramps again, and for a moment I'm not sure it'll stick. Then it settles.

"Tell me what happened." Her eyes are soft. "Emma? Her stomach hurt? Before—?"

All I can do is nod.

Her hands are on my hands, on my thighs. She's holding them tight and still, and I wonder what my hands were doing before she pinned them down. Slowly her hands move to my back, her arms around me now. Tight and warm.

"Tell me."

The truth has been pent up so long, I'm surprised by how easy it is to speak it aloud. "She was on the Pill. A new one. There was a clotting risk. She knew. It was right there in the side effects small print. Which I never read."

"She probably never read it, either," Jessa says quietly. "I never do. We feel immortal, like the words don't apply to us."

I'll never know—never know if she saw and ignored the risk, or like Jessa's suggesting, never looked risk in the eye at all. None of us will ever know.

"A blood clot moved to her lungs." My chest heaves. "She woke up and said her stomach hurt. Here." I show her, high and tight under my ribs. "I told her it was heartburn. Or a muscle cramp." My voice breaks. "Or stomach flu."

"And you didn't go to the ER." Jessa's voice is against my ear, like an accusation, except it's not. It's gentle, and without judgment.

"I rolled over and went back to sleep. I slept through her pain." The awful feelings roll through me, under my ribs, like old useless sympathy.

Jessa's breath brushes my skin, her hands gentle, patting. Stroking. "It wasn't your fault. It *wasn't*."

"Actually, it was."

She reaches up and wipes tears away. My tears, which I hadn't been aware of.

She shakes her head. "Most of the time, it's heartburn, or a muscle cramp, or stomach flu. You didn't know."

"I should have known."

"No. It was a mistake," she says. "People make mistakes."

"Someone I loved died because of my mistake."

She reaches up and wipes more tears away, but more keep falling. "Oh, Clark," she says, and tightens her arms around me, whispering, "shh, shh, shh." Holding me, rocking me, while the sobs roll out of me like waves breaking on the shore.

34

JESSA

I hold him while he cries, and the tenderness I feel is so big and so bright that I finally, finally understand.

This might have started as fake dating, but I really love him.

This man who is crying, in my arms, for another woman.

I have terrible timing.

Still, there is nothing I can do about the way I feel, so I wrap my arms tighter and bury my face in his hair and try to give him every ounce of comfort I have. The warmth of my body, the steadiness of my arms, whatever I can do to ease his pain. Later I will think about what I need to do to save myself.

We fall asleep on the couch, and when I wake up, he's gone.

And pretty much, I know right then.

But still, I try.

Me: *Hey. Feeling any better?*
Clark: *Had a banana, nothing happened, think I'm good*
Me: *Want me to come over with chicken soup?*

Clark: [-]
Me: *Or, I make a mean Korean rice porridge?*
Clark: *Getting ready for a trip. Gone tomorrow am thru Thurs*

Okay. Not gonna freak out. He's taking a trip, he's going to go dark for the next three days. It's not personal. It's the nature of the woods.

THREE DAYS LATER.

Me: *Hey, how was the trip? Wanna Netflix and chill?*
Clark: *Busy tonight. Another time?*

He just got back. He needs some time to unwind.

And we had a big, intense moment. He needs time to process.

Jessa, you're the world's worst liar. You can't even lie to yourself.

Me: *Not sure what's going on with you, but* [deleted]
Me: *Hey, can we talk?* [deleted]
Me: *I know what happened was really intense for you, but* [deleted]

Me: *Miss you.*
Clark: [-]

After that, I quit lying to myself. He's blowing me off. But it takes me another day to gather the courage to do what I know I need to do.

Get some answers.

I go to his apartment and knock.

And there he is. He pulls the door open and stands there staring at me, like I'm the last thing he thought he'd see. Which is absurd of course, because when you don't answer someone's texts for days, you can safely expect her to show up and demand to know why.

I was figuring he'd look the way he did when he left my apartment, like something a vampire had just finished up with. But actually, he looks good. Ruddy cheeked and healthy, a young Viking in the prime of life.

"Are you really going to ghost me?" I ask him. "Or, sorry, I mean *fake* ghost me, because you can't *really* ghost me since we weren't *really* dating."

I don't mean it to come out so sharp and brittle, but that's how it sounds. Like icicles falling on iced-over ground.

He pulls the door all the way open, inviting me in with the gesture, but his body is folded inward, closed. "I'm sorry," he says. Just that. No, *I didn't know what to say,* or, *I was trying to deal with big feelings,* or, *I was feeling weird about having a complete meltdown,* or, *I'm still in love with Emma.*

I step past him into the foyer, hit with the memories of the times we barely made it past the door. He doesn't touch me, so I reach out and put a hand on his arm. He flinches from it.

"Clark."

He's not looking at me.

"Are we—I don't even know how to ask this. Are we—" *breaking up?*

Can you break up if you weren't dating?

"I'm just trying to figure out what to expect," I say. "We said we'd keep up the fake dating until the wedding. But there's also—the sex."

I think about the other night, the sex that felt so powerful and so real. I think about how I wanted us to be face-to-face —but maybe he needed not to look at me. Maybe he needed me not to be me. Maybe he was thinking of *her*.

"I guess I thought—I thought maybe the sex was—" I don't know how to end the sentence. "Real. And the way it made me feel. Because it made me feel so much, Clark. It made me feel like this—" I gesture at us. At all of it. "Like this was real."

He clears his throat. "It was real," he says, and his gaze trips to mine. There's a glimmer in his eyes, a reflection of the longing I'm feeling.

Something in my chest grips hard, trying to hold onto this, the look in his eyes, even though I heard it. *Was.* Past tense.

He opens his mouth, and hope flares bright.

Then the glimmer in his eyes goes dark. He shakes his head.

"It was too real," he says.

And even then, even when he says "was," even when he says "too," I'm still a little bit hopeful.

But then he closes his eyes and the pain on his face is so palpable that I lose my breath.

"I can't," he says.

He shakes his head.

"I'm not ready."

And there it is.

There isn't room for someone else.

There isn't room for me.

"Clark." My voice cracks but doesn't break.

This shouldn't feel like a surprise, Jessa Olsen. You can't build something real on a foundation of fake. You can't start with a lie, pile truths on top, and pray it'll hold together. And you can't ask a man who tells you from the very beginning that he doesn't have it in him to love again to change his mind, just because you lost your way, somewhere in the fiction.

He looks away, his gaze skating up along the far edge of the room, remote. "You're leaving anyway."

"Yeah," I say. "I'm leaving anyway."

35

CLARK

I'm sitting at the bar in Oscar's when a hand clamps down on my shoulder.

Kane.

He sits down beside me, scrutinizes my whiskey, and orders his own.

One of the many nice things about having four brothers and a sister is that even if you want to drink yourself to death alone, there's usually someone trying to keep you from doing it.

"Jill texted Amanda and Amanda texted me," Kane says, confirming both that you can't hope to escape yourself in a town like Rush Creek and that my siblings are really excellent human beings.

"And you came out of the goodness of your heart," I say, one eyebrow raised.

He sighs and ducks his head, wrapping his hand tighter around his whiskey, and despite the misery that has dogged me since the hospital, I can't hide a smile. "The girl in Vegas?" I hazard.

"I can't get her out of my fucking head," he admits.

"That good, huh?"

"I know this sounds fucking nuts," he says, "but it wasn't just sex."

I raise my eyebrows. "That sounds pretty fucking nuts. You screwed her in a bathroom in a hotel and you don't know her name."

"We connected," he says helplessly.

Even though I think Kane's a hopeless romantic with too little life experience under his belt, I also kinda know what he's talking about. "Sometimes your dick knows the truth your heart's too fucked up to see," I concede. "Don't quote me on that. I don't want it on my gravestone."

"You're a poet, Clark," Kane says darkly.

We drink in silence for a bit.

Kane lifts his head. Sighs. "She was my type so hard. My *downfall* type." He closes his eyes. "Manic pixie dream girl all the way. I'm such a sucker for that type."

I almost interrupt him, because if that's true, why does he always go after the girl next door type? His last few girlfriends have had both feet so firmly on the ground, I'm surprised they ever leave it.

"I mean, Clark, you should have fucking seen her. Wild red hair, big green eyes, long lashes, all ethereal woodland fairy beauty. And I told you, she said she never stays put. Moves around—"

"Wait," I say. "Wait."

I think of the woman I met the other night in the bar, the one who renovates RVs for a living. I might have described her that way. What are the chances, though? Vegas is packed to the gills with dreamers of all sorts. It's the slim-to-none-est possibility that she's the same woman who fucked Kane in a hotel bathroom.

But worth trying.

"I might have met her," I say. "I chatted with a woman by that description, the night before you hooked up with her. She renovates RVs. I got her business card—"

But as the words are coming out of my mouth, I remember.

"Oh, shit," I say.

"What?" Kane demands.

"Buck ate that business card. I brought some Vegas clothes to the dry cleaner in the Wilder van, and the card ended up on the floor, and then on the next trip Buck ate it and of course got sick all over everything."

"That fucking dog!"

"I think—her name was a flower. And I remember thinking it was edible."

Kane snorts.

"God, I'm sorry, Kane! I lost the card and I can't remember. Maybe I could track her down, assuming she's left any imprint on the interwebz, which she must have, right? How many women could there be who renovate RVs and are named for edible flowers?"

Kane sets his glass down. "No," he says definitely. "Don't look for her. Promise you won't. No more manic pixies. Or I'll end up like an art house movie hero, chasing her down train tracks, yelling her name as she jumps and hitches a ride far, far away, and the train pulls out of my reach."

"That's a very specific, vivid fantasy you've got there. Ever thought about writing movie scripts?"

He closes his eyes and drops his head into his hands.

I toss back my whiskey. When I finish, he's lifted his head and is watching me. I signal the bartender for two more.

"What about you?" he asks.

"What about me?"

"Did Jessa dump your ass?"

The sick feeling that's dogged me all week rolls over me again, and I chase my second whiskey with a third, setting the glass down hard. "No one dumped anyone's ass."

Kane watches, thoughtful. "Well, something happened. You were your old self in Vegas, and now you're Mopey Boy Blue."

Where does Kane get this shit? "Mopey Boy Blue?"

"We all noticed. You didn't say a word at dinner the other night. And she wasn't there. Amanda said she couldn't make it. Something with work. And then she and Lucy exchanged girl-glances and Lucy said something about being glad they hadn't done the seating chart yet."

My stomach curdles, and whatever expression flits across my face, Kane sees it. "What happened?" he demands.

"Cone of silence?"

"I don't know what the fuck that means," he says.

I air-draw a cone shape around us. "It means, basically, you don't tell Amanda."

He squints.

"Come on, Kane. I know you two are besties, but do you want to know or not?"

"I want to know," he says sulkily.

It's highly probable that Amanda will interrogate the truth out of Kane if she finds out we drank together tonight, but I'm three whiskeys in and can't give a shit anymore.

"It was an act. We were fake dating."

It's the most honest I've been with Kane in weeks. Months. And yet, as the words come out of my mouth, they feel like a lie. What the hell is that?

"The whole time?"

I shake my head. "Yes. Or no. I don't know. It got complicated at the end. Fake dating and real—" I'd been about to say "real fucking" but it's the wrong word for what Jessa and I did. "It got complicated," I say again, lamely.

Kane gives me a sideways, thoughtful look. "It usually does. Why the faking?" he asks. "Why not just date her? You clearly liked her."

"Everyone wanted me to move on, but I wasn't... I'm not ready."

"So you lied to all of us and messed with the feelings of both of you instead," Kane says sagely. "Makes perfect sense."

"Shut up," I say.

"Too much truth?" Kane inquires.

"I was perfectly happy here by myself with my whiskey and my idiocy," I tell him.

That's another lie, and I know it.

"So what's going to happen?" he says.

"Nothing. Nothing's going to happen. She's going to move to the East Coast and do event planning stuff, and I'm going to stay here and..."

"Drink yourself into oblivion?"

"I'm fine," I tell him.

"Uh-huh," he says.

36

JESSA

I'm supposed to work with Lucy and Amanda on the seating chart for the Wilder wedding this afternoon, and every time I think about it, a chasm opens up in my gut.

I don't know if they know that Clark and I broke up.

I don't know if they know why.

I don't know if they'll ask me questions, or if so, about what.

This is the first time since Clark's and my conversation a week ago that I've had to confront a member of the Wilder family face-to-face, in person, and it sucks.

The last week has passed in a blur. Between the Wilder wedding and the Darman-Stevens wedding, the workload is epic. I fall into bed each night exhausted and wake up early to start again. My brain is locked onto details, and everything else exists in a vague fog.

I'm thankful for the fog, because it means I haven't really been able to think about Clark. Or the big, aching spot in the middle of my chest.

I find Imani in her office, where I sit facing her, and say, "I have to ask you a big favor."

"Shoot." No hesitation.

"I need you to switch with me and take lead on the Wilder wedding. I'll take lead on Darman-Stevens."

She squints at me. "You *hate* that wedding," she says. "And anyway, what the fuck? It'll take us days to debrief each other. Not to mention you're already in the spin up to Wilder—me taking over right now would be like changing horses midrace." Her eyes comb my face, and her mouth falls open. "Ohh… no. No, nope, nope. I am not swapping weddings with you because you made it all complicated. You're a big girl. You can ride this one out."

"I didn't make it complicated. Clark made it complicated."

She curls her fingers in a give-me-the-story gesture.

I tell her everything she's missed since the last update—what happened in the lagoon at Edelweiss, our time together in Vegas, and the night we had transcendent sex and he tried to get me to go to the ER for stomach flu. How it was fake and then it was fake plus real and then it got way too real for Clark.

How I fell in love just as he made it clear there was no room in his heart for me.

When I'm done, when I've told her about how Clark said he *couldn't*, Imani levels her most searching gaze on me. "And after he said he wasn't ready, you said…?"

"I mean, I can't literally remember what words came out of my mouth."

"The gist," she says impatiently.

"I guess… I said… *okay*?"

Her eyes get huge. "Seriously?!"

"What should I have said? I mean, he's right. I am leaving."

She crosses her arms. "But you don't have to leave."

"Madison and Ferris need me."

She cocks her head. "Do they? Or are you leaving Rush Creek because you're ashamed of making mistakes that weren't even really your mistakes?"

"I don't know what you're talking about."

Her eyes are kind. "I know Reuben humiliated you, and I know it feels hard to stick around when everyone knows you as the woman in the book, but the truth is, everyone who knows the story's true also knows it was the lowest, most asshole possible thing to do. No one's on Reuben's side." She scrunches up her face, considering that. "Well, except maybe some middle-aged professors who are using his book as a text in their boring-ass American Literature of Dull Misogynistic White Guys classes."

I can't help smiling at that.

"And yeah, sure, it was a bad day when you chose to hire Bonnie the thief, but you think no one's ever done that before? Hardly. So yeah, we've had to rebuild the business's image, but look at us! We're doing great. We're almost back to where we were before, and on firmer ground than last time. But no, you need to walk away because wedding planning suddenly isn't really your dream, even though you've been planning weddings in your head since you were a little girl."

"I'm not walking away because of Bonnie!"

"Yes! You! Are! And you're walking away from Clark because you believe the line Reuben sold you, that you're not lovable enough for the long haul, and so as soon as Clark freaked out a little bit, which by the way is fucking normal because the guy lost his *wife* and he thought he was going to lose you, too, you decided you were no competition for his dead wife. Even though, and I cannot stress this enough, people do not freak out like Clark freaked out unless they're batshit crazy in love."

"Wait, what?" I demand.

"You got sick and he freaked the hell out. Lost his shit, yelled, tried to haul you bodily to the ER, puked, and cried. That does not sound like a guy who *can't*. That sounds to me like a guy who already *has* and is scared out of his fucking wits. Which is *normal*, because he lost the last woman he fell in love with."

"He's not in love with me."

"He is," she says. "And if you weren't so busy being worried about doing it wrong and making a mistake, you'd dig your heels in and tell him so."

I'm still shaking my head. "Anyway," I tell her, "It doesn't matter how he feels about me, because he *can't*."

She lifts her hands to her face, one on either side of her nose, and stares at me over the steeple. Then she sighs.

"Maybe," she says. "But if you're being totally honest with yourself, neither can you."

I don't deny it.

She watches my face for a long time, then heaves a big sigh.

"Okay," she says. "If you need to trade, I'll trade."

37

CLARK

My brothers and I are picking up our tuxes and getting a last-minute recheck on the fit.

We're in a room of mirrors, with five Wilders, plus Heath, all tuxed-up and reflected from all sides. It's a little terrifying, like some weird-ass black-and-white kaleidoscope. There are two tailors, a young, bearded Black guy and a middle-aged white mom-type, scrambling around, checking the break of our pants legs over our shoes, muttering to themselves, and spitting pins.

Meanwhile, all my brothers are posting photos of themselves to Insta and tagging their significant others.

"Hashtag them #wilderadventures," Gabe reminds everyone. "And #wilderwedding."

"Seriously?" Easton demands. "People are not going to book trips because you're getting married."

"Right," Gabe says. "The idea is they're going to book trips because we look damn good in our tuxes. And because they'll associate the idea of getting married in Rush Creek with the idea of going on an adventure."

"You sound like Lucy," Easton says with a big sigh; but he taps a few more times, presumably hashtagging his posts.

I'm the only one who doesn't have his phone out.

Brody pokes me and says, "Send one to Jessa."

Kane gives him a look, and Brody, oblivious to recent events, says, "What?! He wants to get some tonight, doesn't he?"

Kane's dirty look doubles down and Brody, who's a clueless guy but not a dick, says, "Oh, *shit*."

"Not gonna happen," I say.

"No. She didn't," says Gabe. "She's going to fuck up the seating chart!"

"Oh, right, *God forbid* someone fuck with the seating chart!" Kane says. Good man.

"But she's leaving you in the lurch." Gabe is gratifyingly outraged on my behalf, even if he's got it all wrong. "And right before the wedding!"

"Why do you assume it's her?" I demand. "Maybe I broke it off."

They all turn to look at me, causing all their infinitely mirrored counterparts to also swivel, a dizzying effect.

"Because we *saw* you with her," Brody says.

Infinity Wilders nod.

"I don't know what you're trying to say." Maybe it's just the head-spinning effect of mirrors, Wilders, and tuxes, but nothing is making sense to me.

"He's saying it was obvious you were really into her," Easton clarifies.

"But he's not," Kane says.

"Kane," I say urgently.

He looks from me to my brothers. "You should just tell them the truth."

"Well, obviously now I have to," I say grumpily.

I turn to the wall of waiting Wilders and admit, "It was an act. We were fake dating."

Infinity eyebrows draw together.

So I tell them how it all got started, trying to stick it to Jessa's cheating ex, defending myself against Amanda, and then how it took on a life of its own.

I get to the part where Jessa got sick. The part where I freaked out and tried to bodily haul her to the ER. And the part where I realized I just couldn't do it again. Couldn't open myself up to her the way she deserved, couldn't fall in love and live in fear that something awful would happen to her.

"I ended it. But it would have ended anyway. She's moving to the East Coast in a few weeks."

Easton says, "Jesus."

Brody says, "I honestly thought you were kidding when you said you were going to fake date to get mom off your back."

Kane says nothing, because he's already had his moment.

And Gabe is staring at me.

"What?" I demand, because this is definitely not the response I expected from him. I was figuring he'd be pissed—on his own behalf, because he doesn't always have a sense of humor about himself, and also on behalf of everyone else I'd deceived: Lucy, Amanda, Hanna, everyone. But he doesn't look pissed. He looks... genuinely baffled.

"You broke up with her so you *wouldn't fall in love with her*?"

"Yeah," I say.

He exchanges looks with my other brothers. All infinity of them.

"What?!" I demand.

"Nothing," he says. "Nothing."

Emma's mom answers the door, salt-and-pepper hair up, and beams at the sight of me.

"Clark!" she says.

"Can I come in?"

"Of course!"

She opens the door and ushers me into the kitchen, where she offers me coffee. I accept—I need something to do with my hands.

"I'm not a hundred percent sure why I'm here," I say.

Her eyes travel over my face. "Whatever it is," she says, "I'm glad to see you."

I realize, then, how much I've missed her. She was a good mother-in-law. I loved—love—her. The realization makes my eyes prickle.

"I think I need—" I stop. "I need to tell you something."

She nods.

"It's my fault. That she died."

She's already shaking her head.

"No, please, let me talk. That night, I knew she was in pain. And I didn't make her go to the ER. I thought it was just a stomachache."

She reaches out and takes both my hands. Hers are warm and firm and solid. She's crying, tears running down her face, and I feel extra shitty for bringing my pain to her. I shouldn't be here. But then she releases my hands, gets up, gets a box of tissues, and brings it back to the table. And I realize I'm crying, too.

I've cried more in the last few days than I did in the weeks after Emma died.

Which should probably tell me something about how stunted my grief was.

Right. *That's* why I'm here. Because I've been stuck, and now I'm coming unstuck. And it hurts, but it's also what I have to do if I'm going to be able to—

Able to love again someday.

Both of us mop our faces.

"Can I tell you a story?" she asks, and plunges in without waiting for a response. "When Emma was in high school, she played basketball. She was pretty good, but she had a terrible mental game. Anything that went wrong? She blamed herself. 'I should have made a better pass in the second quarter,' 'I shouldn't have let myself get stripped in the third,' 'I shouldn't have missed that free throw at the end.'

"So finally I figured out how to explain it to her so she could understand. A basketball game, it's made up of so many moments. Not just points, but moments. Split-second decisions, tiny little choices. You feel like yours are the ones that matter, because they're yours, but the truth is, it's a sea of moments, and yours are just drops.

"Someone did the initial science that led to that pill. Someone engineered the specific formula that created that pill. Someone manufactured that pill."

Her voice is matter-of-fact. Level. I can see the lines of grief in her face, but she's not angry. She's just stating the truth.

"Someone let it go to market when it did. Someone did shitty science, and someone let the shitty science slide through. And someone forgot to mention to her daughter that when she was eighteen, she'd had a minor blood clot in her leg after an airline flight, because it was such a non-event that it didn't seem worth bringing up. Until it was too late, and then it seemed like the most important thing in the world."

I almost fall off my seat.

"I'm sorry I didn't tell you," she says. "I was ashamed, and I didn't realize how much you were blaming yourself. If I had, I would have told you right away, so we could work through it together instead of alone."

She has my hands in hers again.

"Maybe we still can?" I say.

She smiles at that.

"I would like that."

We're silent for a moment. I pick up my coffee and drain the cup, then set it down.

"Clark," she says.

"Mmm-hmm."

"I'm sure you know we live in a town where there are no secrets."

My eyes fly to her face.

"There is a rumor afoot that you have a new girlfriend."

I watch the emotions move over her face, and I know them all: sadness, that there ever had to be anyone other than Emma; anger, that Emma lost the world and we lost her; and a backwards, vicarious envy: I should have been Emma's and Emma's alone, and someone else has what she deserved.

Had.

"Had," I say aloud. "It didn't work out."

She watched me quietly. More than anyone else, I feel like she can see through me. Like she understands what I'm fighting through.

"I'm not going to say something dumb, like Emma would want you to be happy."

I can't help it; I grin at the aggravation in her voice. We've both heard plenty of platitudes in the last two years.

"And I'm not going to lie—I'm a jealous bitch, and I'm pissed that someone else might ever get you for a son-in-law. I lost that, too."

Her voice breaks, and I stand up, abruptly, cross to her side of the table, and wrap my arms around her.

"You did *not*," I say. "I just needed some time."

When she stops crying, she says, "You are a good man, Clark Wilder. And it would be a fucking waste of a good man if you crawled into a hole and refused to come out. That is all I am going to say."

38

JESSA

My bags are packed. My stuff's been shipped, or in a few cases, sold.

The Darman-Stevens wedding was last weekend. It came off without a hitch, and even though I had to fight back the urge to roll my eyes about a thousand times, I also had tears on my cheeks when Kyle slid the ring onto Brandi's finger and they recited the vows they'd written.

The Wilder wedding is this coming weekend, but I won't be here for that. I'm leaving town earlier than I'd planned. Imani took over The Best Day, and I'll be in Philly, with Madison and Ferris, keeping them company until their surrogate goes into labor.

I'm sleeping the next few nights at Imani's, and then I'll head to the airport.

I wheel my bags to the door, just as someone knocks on it. It's still about twenty minutes early for Imani to pick me up, and Imani is always five minutes late, so I'm not surprised when I open the door and it's not her.

It's Amanda.

"Hey," she says, when I open the door. "I have some questions for you."

I invite her in. Despite everything, despite the weight in my belly, the tightness in my chest, and the heavy sadness that's followed me around since Clark broke things off, I am so glad to see her, and I tell her so. Unfortunately, my voice shakes and my eyes fill up with tears, giving me away completely.

She throws her arms around me. "You silly! Did you think we would stop being friends if you stopped dating Clark?" She pulls back for a look, then dives into the hug again. "Nope. I like you *way* too much for that. No. You are stuck with me. I'm sorry about that, but that's how it is." And she hugs me even harder.

So of course I start crying. Like, really crying.

"Oh, hon," Amanda says, like the mom of three and friend to all she is. "Cry it out, babe. Let it all out. And then explain what the fuck is going on, because I have heard some wild versions of reality lately."

"Okay," Amanda says, when I'm done explaining. "I have to be honest, I still don't totally understand. He pretended you were together to give Reuben shit. That part I get. And of course I get the part where he messed with my head. That doesn't require any explanation—or at least not any beyond "Wilder siblings." But you're going to have to explain to me about 'fake dating' and 'real sex.'"

She hooks some seriously deep finger quotes, both her neatly arched eyebrows tipping up.

We're sitting across from each other, each of us on one of my hard-sided suitcases. It's not the comfiest seating, but it's all I've got at the moment.

I take a deep breath. "It's just—the relationship part was fake, but we kept—things kept—the chemistry was off the—"

She waves a hand, face scrunched up. "Yeah, yeah, don't elaborate, *please*, he is still my brother." Her expression smooths, but there are deep lines between her eyebrows. "So what were you faking, exactly? The feelings?"

I think about that for a moment. "Well, I was supposed to be faking the feelings," I say. "But then the sex was real, and then the feelings got real, too. You know. How they do."

"Yes," Amanda says. "Yes, I do know." She thinks about it a moment more. "So it was real sex and real feelings."

"For me," I emphasize. "But not for him. It was fake feelings for him."

"Really?" Amanda asks, eyeing me suspiciously "Because it did *not* look fake to me. At all. And here's the thing."

She crosses her arms.

"I know my brothers pretty well. And to a man?" She raises her eyebrows. "They're *terrible* fakers."

39

CLARK

"Clark," my mother says in her scariest, most parental voice. "A word with you."

It's the morning of Gabe and Lucy's wedding. We're all at the church, getting dressed, and she has appeared in the doorway of the groom's room, where my brothers and I are gathered, admiring our tux-clad selves. There are a lot fewer mirrors here than at the tailors, but mirrors there are. It's about thirty minutes to go-time—or maybe a little less.

Gabe is surprisingly calm. I thought all guys got cold feet before their weddings, but Gabe seems utterly unfazed. That man was born to be in charge.

I'm slow getting to my feet, and my mother glares at me. Casting a "save me!" glance back at my brothers and getting absolutely nothing useful in return, I slink out into the hallway and follow her out of earshot of the others. Although they probably have a surveillance drone on me. They've been watching me all weekend like hawks, as if they think I'm going to have a breakdown.

They're not completely wrong.

It has been hard.

But not for the reason they think.

Do I wish Emma were here?

God, yes. Of course. I wish the world had never taken her away from me.

But the person I miss with a fierceness I can't even fathom is Jessa.

She should be here.

Instead, she's catching a flight to the East Coast early this evening, or so Imani told me when I finally let myself ask where Jessa was.

Last night at the rehearsal dinner, I made conversation with friends and relatives, desperately wishing she were on my arm. Wishing she was laughing with me at the weird awkward things people say when they're making conversation, wishing I could see her face brimming with feeling at the heartfelt moments, like when Gabe and Lucy gave a speech about how much they loved their families.

But she wasn't there, and I made it through.

Now it's Wedding Day.

And my mom is *pissed*. Eyes flashing, hands waving.

"Fake!" she says. "Fake! Clark!"

Uh-oh.

"I was going on to Hanna about how bad I felt for you, not having Emma and having just broken up with Jessa, and how it must be hard for you even to have Imani running things today instead of Jessa, and she looks like she's going to throw up on my shoes, and then she blurts out that it was never real to begin with. That you faked the whole thing."

I blink. "Uh. I, uh."

"Clark Wilder, I raised you better than that! You should

have just told me you wanted me to shut up about starting dating again! You went to these lengths to keep me off your back?"

My mother can be mild-mannered right up until she isn't, and then she's a force to be reckoned with. That's actually how Lucy came into our lives.

Do not mess with my mother.

I mean, ultimately my mother was right. About the need for someone like Lucy and her great business ideas. And about the general awesomeness of Lucy. But still. It was a messy few weeks.

Maybe that's the Wilder way. We get there eventually, but sometimes the journey is messy.

You could argue that that's the nature of adventure.

My mother, having vented her frustration, is staring at me with sad, betrayed green eyes, and the last thing I want to do is hurt this woman who gave us everything even after she lost *her* everything. So I tell her the absolute fucking truth:

"I didn't do it to keep you off my back."

Her face softens. "Then why *did* you do it?"

Why?

So easy.

"I did it for Jessa," I say.

My mother tilts her head.

"Reuben, her creep-o ex, pissed me off so bad. And Jessa—"

I'm remembering things.

How much I needed not to want her the night of the literacy fundraiser.

How instantly I came to her defense when I saw that Reuben still wanted to wound her.

How much I didn't want her to hurt when Reuben and Corinna were making noisy love in the clearing.

How ready, willing, and able I was to make the kissing—and the touching, and the lovemaking—real.

How totally fucking terrified I was when she was in pain.

Because.

Because—

The answer is right there, demanding my attention, even as my mind is trying to push it back.

It would be a fucking waste of a good man if you crawled into a hole and refused to come out.

But that is exactly what I did, isn't it? Crawled into a foxhole, made a helmet out of my arms, and sang *la-la-la*.

My mother is watching me with a soft expression. It's very different from the amusement on Gabe's face at the tux fitting, but it's also the same.

"I wanted to fix everything for her. I wanted to make everything okay for her."

And the thing is?

I can't stop wanting that.

"You love her," my mother says, very softly. Very gently. She understands, I'm pretty sure, that even two weeks ago, I couldn't have heard those words.

But right now?

It's the first thing in days—no, weeks—no months—that feels completely and totally true.

"Yeah," I say, and I laugh. Out loud. "I love her."

"Oh, Clark," she says.

"I gotta—" I can't even finish the sentence, but that's okay. She waves me off. "Go."

I race back to the groom's room. "Gabe—"

I catch a glimpse of myself in the mirror and see one wild-eyed man. Thank God there aren't infinity of me.

"I know I'm supposed to be your best man, but I have to go."

His mouth falls open. "What the fuck?"

"I have to go get Jessa. She's on her way to the East Coast."

His expression changes utterly. And, to my shock, he starts to laugh.

"Oh, man. Your timing, Clark. And I thought I was an idiot." Then he waves me off, just like my mom had. "Go," he says. "Go get her."

"I might miss the wedding," I whisper.

He shrugs. "There'll be video."

"But I'm supposed to be your best man."

He grins. Waves a hand around the room, gesturing at our brothers, who are all watching me warily, like I might explode.

"I've got spares."

I LOOK AT MY WATCH. It's 3:06.

My fingers flying over my phone, I call up today's flights. She has to be flying out of Portland International. There's one evening flight to the East Coast, at 6:30.

I google the directions. Three hours, twenty-two minutes. Holy shit.

"There's no way I can make it. Flight's at six thirty."

"If you leave right now, you'll make it," Brody says. "I've done it in under three in a pinch."

"Yeah, well, my car doesn't have hyperdrive."

Once a bad boy, always a speed demon—although he's gotten a lot better since he has Rachel and Justin in his life.

"Just don't drive like a grandma, Grandma," he flings back.

"Stop fighting and go!"

That's the Gabriel Wilder voice of reason.

I fly out of the groom's room and down the hall.

"Clark!" a voice says, moments before a hand lands on my arm. I look up to see Rachel, holding a big cardboard box. "I have the boutonnieres! I need you to pin them on the groomsmen."

"Can you do it?" I ask, but she shakes her head. "Lucy stepped on the hem of her dress and someone needs to stitch it. Imani and Amanda are dealing with something that went wrong with the drinks, so the dress situation is on me." She shoves the boutonnieres in my arms and races away.

I look at my watch. 3:10.

I hurry back to the groom's room with the box.

"What the fuck are you doing still here?" Gabe demands.

"Someone needs to pin the boutonnieres on," I say.

"I got it," Brody says, holding out his arms for the box.

"I love you, man," I say.

"Save it for the girl," he says.

"I still love you."

He claps a hand on my back. "Love you, too, dude. Now fucking *go!*"

I'm back down the hall, heart pounding even harder this time.

It'll save time if I cut through the nave, so I do, then up the aisle, past a startled minister. There are a few people already in their seats, reading their programs or fussing with their phones. An usher is seating Rachel's parents, brother, and grandmother; I fly by them.

"Clark," Connor says, hand on my arm. "Can I grab you for a second?"

3:12.

"Uh, yeah, what is it, dude?" I ask, my heart pounding out the seconds of time I'm losing on my quest.

"I'm just wondering if you're hiring at all. For any of the wilderness trips. We don't have to talk about it now or anything—"

"Yeah," I say. "No. Yes, hiring, no, can't talk about it now. We'll talk tomorrow. I promise. I fucking promise."

"You okay, man?" he asks, taking in my face. "Everything okay with the wedding and all? Gabe's not having cold feet or anything, is he? No big last-minute crises?"

"No!" I howl. "Everything's fine!"

He puts his hands up. "Whoa. Okay. You sure you're—?"

"Gotta go!"

"Clark?"

I ignore him, race the final few steps to the back of the nave, and push open the doors.

Now I'm in the lobby. There are a few people milling around out there, too, and a single friend of Amanda's who's hit on me a few times.

3:13.

I reach the big church doors, with their huge ornate handles, grasp them, pull them open.

Jessa is standing there.

40

JESSA

I thought that Clark Wilder in a suit was the pinnacle of hot, but now I have seen him in a tux.

Viking in a tux. It is a thing.

His beard is neatly trimmed again. His shirt is crisp and white, a sharp contrast with his gold-tanned skin. His big shoulders and chest fill out the shirt and jacket, his body narrowing in that spectacularly sexy upside-down male triangle to a trim waist and hips. But his thigh muscles challenge the fit of his slacks, and that's enough to take the joy I feel at seeing him and turn it into something naughtier.

"What's—where are you going?" I ask him, at the same time he demands, "What are you doing here?"

"You first," I say.

"I was—" He hesitates, and something shy comes into his expression. "I was going to get you."

"You—what? What about Gabe and Lucy's wedding?"

"There's video," he says.

"But—" I sputter. "You're the best man."

"Gabe said he has spares."

I'm slowly starting to realize that he is totally serious.

"You were going to miss your brother's wedding to come to the airport—to do what?"

That seems to stop him.

"Uh," he says. "I guess—to ask you—to *beg* you—not to move to the East Coast."

"Really?" I ask, beyond delighted. "Really, really? Like not fake really?"

"Really, really, *really*, really," he says, a slow smile blooming on his face.

I can't keep the smile off my face, either. Clark Wilder was coming to the airport to *beg* me not to move to the East Coast.

(In his tux.)

Omigod omigod omigod.

I almost wish I'd gone to the airport, too, because can you imagine it? Big Viking in a tux begging li'l ol' me *in an airport*?

Although this is pretty good. People are coming up to the church from their cars, and since we're still standing in the open doors of the church, people in the lobby have all stopped what they're doing to watch the drama in progress.

"But you're not at the airport," Clark says, as if this fact is just slowly dawning on him.

I shake my head. "I didn't go."

"Why...?"

"Well," I say. "I realized I had unfinished business on this side of the country."

"And what's that?" he asks, his smile getting bigger.

"I stranded you without a date to this wedding."

His eyes track my body—my pale pink dress, my high heels. Then back up to take in my hair and makeup.

"You're so beautiful," he says, and the awe in his voice makes tears come into my eyes.

"You okay with that?" I ask him. "I know there was a time when you didn't want to think I was pretty."

"I'm *so* okay with that," he says, his voice dropping into the register that makes it rub, velvet-nap, against my nerve endings. He leans close, so his breath brushes my ear, lighting up every cell in my body.

"I was wrong," he murmurs. "I *can*. I'm ready."

My pulse goes nuts; I have to pull back to look at him, to make sure he means it. His eyes, full of heat and love, tell me he does. So does his smile, big and full and absolutely real.

He ducks close again, his lips touching the shell of my ear, then sweeping along my jaw until he catches my mouth in a long, sweet, hungry kiss.

Then he wraps his arms around me and pulls me tight to him, his body already showing me how much he's missed me.

Our audience applauds. "Double wedding!" someone calls.

Right. *Wedding.*

"You should, um, probably get back in there," I say.

"Oh, geez, yeah," he says. He drops a kiss on my mouth, brief but fierce, and books it back inside.

I find my way into the pews. There's no bride's side and groom's side at this wedding because to know a Wilder is to love a Wilder, and I'm surrounded by people who are beaming and thrilled to be here, talking about the adorable story of how Lucy came to town and turned Gabe's world upside down.

A few moments later, the bridesmaids and groomsmen walk down the aisle, two by two, and take their places.

Clark's eyes find mine, and the smile that crosses his face lights up my chest.

Amanda, Rachel, and Hanna, look beautiful in their lilac bridesmaids' dresses. Brody obviously can't tear his eyes away from Rachel. And Easton—

Well, I'm sure if you asked Easton, he'd say he's just shocked to see how nice Hanna cleans up.

And maybe that's true.

The music changes. The door of the nave opens. And Lucy steps in, on the arms of Adele and Gregg.

She looks like—

Well, she looks like a bride.

You know. All in white, hair piled on her head, lots of makeup, and so aglow that it's hard to tear your eyes away.

But I do. I look at Clark to see if he sees it, too.

Except he's not looking at Lucy. He's looking at me—with so much love in his eyes that it's impossible to mistake it for anything else.

Or as intended for anyone else.

I start crying then, and I don't stop until Lucy and Gabe run back up the aisle, hands clasped, bells ringing.

Guess I'm not as much of a cynic as I thought.

41

CLARK

Jessa and I dance a *lot*. We dance to all the oldies and the fast stuff, and we dance to the slow stuff that lets us put our arms around each other and breathe in each other's scent and just *hold* each other.

It also lets us talk a little bit, and there's some stuff to talk about. Like, "What made you change your mind?"

That's what Jessa asks me the first time we're alone-ish, on the dance floor, with no one fist-bumping us (Easton), or hugging the hell out of us (Amanda, Rachel, Brody), or giving us quizzical side-eye (Hanna), or not even noticing we exist because they have eyes only for each other (Gabe and Lucy—as well they should).

"What made you change your mind?"

"The short version is that I realized I was in love with you, and everything else stopped mattering."

Her breath catches. "Clark," she whispers.

"It's true." But I actually want to tell her the long version, because I understand that she needs more. She needs to know exactly how much she means to me, and how sure I am of this. "I think it started with something Kane said."

"Which was?"

"Well, he wanted to know why I didn't just date you, when I clearly liked you. And I think that was the first time I realized why I'd done it. The 'fake' part. It was because it made my feelings for you safe. I wanted to have those feelings, but they were scaring the shit out of me. So I put a box around them. And the box was 'fake dating.'"

She squeezes me tighter, resting her cheek against my shoulder, which I fucking love. She fits perfectly there.

"And then there was something Gabe didn't say."

"Something he *didn't* say?"

"Yeah. He said, 'You broke up with her so you *wouldn't fall in love with her*?' And then he and my brothers gave each other these incredulous looks. I just figured they thought I was a straight up idiot."

I step back and cup her face in my hands. She's especially pretty tonight, lashes long and dark, cheeks pink, lips red and glossy. But she's always beautiful to me.

"It took something my mom said to me to help me realize that, actually, my brothers thought I was a particular kind of idiot."

Her eyes are big, her lips curved with suppressed humor. "Yeah?"

"Yeah. The kind who was trying so hard not to fall in love with you that I missed the fact that I already had."

"Oh," she says, a soft exhalation.

"I love you," I whisper.

She looks at me, her eyes shining.

"I love you, too, Clark Wilder."

I bend my head and kiss her, and she kisses me back, hungrily, her tongue sneaking out.

"Family show," I remind her, as her whole body curves into mine.

"Right. Right." She draws back a little as the music segues into Ed Sheeran's "Thinking Out Loud," then settles back into my arms.

I don't tell her about going to see Emma's mom. There's plenty of time for that story, and it's OK for Emma not to be here right now. She'll always be a part of me, but tonight is Jessa's and my night.

"What about you?" I ask. "What made you come back, even though I was being a total and complete tool?"

"Total and complete is maybe a little harsh?" she offers, but she's laughing. I don't think she *actually* thinks it's too harsh.

"Short version?" she asks.

"Can I have the summary and the whole long story, same as I gave you?"

She nods. "Short version is, I realized that even if you weren't ready for me now, I wanted to be here when you were."

For some reason, that knocks me off my feet. I don't know —maybe it's just part of how I feel, like she's taken me where I am this whole time. Not trying to push, not trying to rush, just getting that it's hard to move past grief the size of mine— even if you want to.

"You okay?" she asks, scrutinizing my face.

"More than."

"Longer version: Imani made me realize that my default reaction to everything is to run away from it. Business giving you trouble? Quit, and do something else. Former marriage humiliating you? Head to the other side of the country. In love with a man who you think might not be ready to love you back? Bail out with a parachute." She winces. "If it were just that, though, I might have still gone. But Imani also pointed out that men don't completely lose their shit when you get sick if they're just not that into you."

I stroke her hair. "Smart one, that Imani," I murmur against the silky strands.

"And Amanda said something super similar. That her brothers were crappy fakers. Which, if I hadn't been so far inside my own freak-out, I would have known, just from knowing you. We didn't pull off that fake dating because either of us was any good at faking it. We pulled it off because we didn't have to fake it."

I pull her closer. "I'm glad you figured that out."

"I'm glad you figured out you were in love with me."

"I'm glad you didn't go."

"I'm glad you were ready."

We've been pressing closer to each other with each declaration, and once again we're not-safe-for-work.

"What would you say—?" I ask, at exactly the same time she says, "What if we—?"

And neither of us has time to finish the sentence before I wrap my hand around hers and haul her off the dance floor and towards the exit.

42

JESSA

I loosen and gently tug at his bowtie, then drop it on the floor of his bedroom.

He lowers the zipper of my dress while his lips follow a line from my ear to my neck to my shoulder, then down my back. He lets the dress fall to the floor, and I turn to face him.

I unbutton his shirt, watching the perfect male beauty that is Clark emerge in the crisp white V. Golden skin, taut over hard muscle, and just the right amount of hair. The hard ridges of his abs.

He takes a sharp breath as I reach around to remove his cummerbund, then drop it on the floor next to the bowtie. His pants are low on his hips, that crisp line of hair disappearing between two deep dives of muscle.

I don't know what happens to the rest of our clothes, because I look up then and I can't look away. There is so much affection and such heat in his gaze, and both are for me.

Me.

So is the kiss he gives me, deep and hungry and forceful, his hands everywhere now, rough and then gentle, like he doesn't know which he wants to be, and he probably doesn't, because I sure as hell don't.

There is a lot of kissing. I lose track of myself until I am just liquid pleasure in his arms. He lays me down on the bed and crawls over me, drawing the column of his condom-sheathed erection up my inner thigh, nudging my legs further apart. Eyes on mine the whole time, so there's not a moment when I don't feel like he sees me.

It's seamless, what happens next. He lowers his mouth to mine and just the touch of his tongue makes me open to him. To his tongue in my mouth and to his fingers, thick at the entrance to my core, while his thumb plays over my clit. He's still kissing me when I feel the tip of his cock take over from his fingers. He's still kissing me when he eases in, so, so slowly, teasing his way past all my defenses.

Kissing and kissing and kissing. He's in me all the way now, as deep as he can get, filling me, stretching me, opening me up to him in every possible way. He supports himself on his arms, the muscles playing under the skin, the curves and cuts and all-male shapes working their magic on some primitive part of my brain. It leaves me breathless, how beautiful he is, braced over me.

"Look at me," he commands, and I know he doesn't mean *keep ogling my chest and arms*, so I raise my eyes to his, and there's something demanding and needy there.

I look into his gray eyes and they aren't holding anything back from me. There's nothing fake about the way he looks at me, like even while he has all of me, he wants more of me. And I want to give it to him. I want to give him absolutely everything; I spread my legs and lift my knees, trying to show him physically what I mean, and then when that isn't enough either, I clutch him in my arms and try to show him that way, and that's *still* not enough. So I kiss him again, and bite him and he curses and laughs and pins me down, holding my wrists, and kissing and biting back.

"I love you," he says. "I love you."

"I love you."

He's holding my wrists which means he can't hold as much of his weight on his arms, which means he's heavier as he thrusts into me, and it's that weight, and the kissing, the biting, the cursing, the laughing, the *loving*, that push me over the edge, and this time it feels like it's enough, it's everything.

EPILOGUE
JESSA—SEVERAL WEEKS LATER

"Gabe," Amanda says sternly.

Gabe looks up from a focused attack on his plate of food to Amanda's expression of mock disapproval.

"What?" he demands.

"You knocked up your wife on your *honeymoon*?"

Amanda's straight up teasing, of course. We've all known Lucy is pregnant since the engagement party. But for the first time, she definitely *looks* pregnant. It might be partly because she's wearing maternity clothes, but I think it's because she has finally popped. She was right. A September wedding was the latest she could go and still fit into Barb's dress.

"I work fast," Gabe says, and then, hilariously, *blushes*.

There isn't much that's cuter than a blushing six-two scruffy mountain man.

I should know. I have one—a mountain man, I mean—and I can make him blush whenever I want.

"Pass the stew, please," Antonio Perez, Rachel's dad says.

He's talking about my mom's yukgaejang. She beams at him.

The Wilders—by which I mean the enormous and ever-growing family with the Wilders at its center—have gathered for a big dinner. My parents were in town, too. They wanted to real-meet Clark, especially once they heard that they were an integral part of the fake-dating story. So they came to Rush Creek for the weekend. When they're done here, I'll head back to Portland with them so all of us can fly East to be on hand for Madison and Ferris's baby's impending birth.

When Barb found out my parents were in town, she insisted that they join us. Which resulted in what might be the best potluck mashup of all time: a huge pot of Wilder spaghetti with meat sauce, *lechon asado* and *platanos*, and my mom's yukgaejang.

Which Clark is steadily demolishing as my mom looks on with approval.

As predicted, Clark and my parents love each other. And maybe it's because my mom loves to feed people and Clark is more than willing to eat every last bite.

But really?

Really, I can't help thinking about what Clark said that day, when we were first trying to agree on a story for our families.

Of course I'd love them, he'd said. *Your parents. If they're anything like you.*

It makes sense. After all, I love the Wilders so freaking much. And yeah, it's because they're kind and funny and always up for an adventure.

But I also love them because they're Clark's, and I love him.

Before dinner, Gabe and Lucy, less than two weeks back from their honeymoon, gave us an old-fashioned slideshow on the big-screen TV in the living room, even though we'd already seen pretty much all of the photos on Instagram. It was still super nice to be part of the family cuddle pile that sprawled all over the couch, several chairs, and an assortment of cushions and beanbags on the floor.

They decided their honeymoon needed to be a hybrid of luxury and adventure, so they went to Hawaii and spent half the time lounging on the beach and half the time hiking and camping. The photos are gorgeous, and made me think Clark and I need to get there as soon as possible.

Not on our honeymoon, of course. I mean, I would like us to have a honeymoon someday, and I think he would, too, but it's only been a few weeks of real everything. The beginning was kinda chaotic, as well. Clark asked me to move in with him, but I said that since we were just getting real with each other, maybe we should give it six months, and he agreed. I was lucky that my landlord hadn't rented my old apartment yet, and even luckier that I was able to reroute the truck carrying most of my belongings back to Rush Creek without having to receive it, empty it, and repack it in Philly. Clark helped me restore everything back to the way it was, more or less, in my apartment, and then we made sure the bed still worked.

Spoiler: It did.

Meanwhile, about a week after the wedding, Clark told me he wanted to cook dinner for me at his place, and as soon as I stepped into the living room, I started to cry.

He'd taken down about half the photos of Emma. And he'd filled all the blank spaces with new framed photos. A gorgeous one of us dancing at the wedding, taken by Kane. One of me helping Clark with the knotted fabric favor box.

One of me chatting with Rachel, Hanna, and Easton at the engagement party—also courtesy of Kane. Me with the girls in Vegas.

You can see on both our faces that we're not faking it.

We were never faking it.

I turned my teary face to him. "I love them. Thank you."

"I love you," he said, and took my hand, and led me to his bedroom.

Of course, now we spend almost every night in either his apartment or mine. I told him we're fake-living-separately.

He laughed. "Yeah. And we're not any better at faking that than anything else we've tried."

Then he kissed me, and we did real stuff for a long time.

After we finish dinner, the Wilders, Perezes, Kennings, Booths, and Olsens make short work of the dishes, and the party drifts out onto the deck and into the backyard. Brody, Heath, and Clark supervise s'mores-making over the firepit with small Kennings and Justin. Barb and Geneva organize the older generations into a sprawling game of bunco that rapidly becomes drunken and raucous. I can hear my parents' voices in the fray, laughing and calling out, and when I look over and catch my dad's eye, he smiles at me—and then gives me a nod of approval.

Not that I need it, as he would be the first to say.

But it's nice how much my family likes him.

Imani, too, is a big Clark fan. When I decided to stay in Rush Creek, I went to her hat in hand to see if she'd be interested in bringing me back on to The Best Day as an employee.

She gave me a long wide-eyed Imani look of disbelief, then said, "Is that really what you want?"

"If you'll have me."

"No," she said. "I mean, don't you want to be my partner?"

My mouth fell open.

"Come on, Jessa, don't be coy. It was your business to begin with."

"Yeah, but I bailed out on you."

"You had a few things to figure out." She shrugged, and then, frowning at me, commanded, "Don't." She shoved a finger in my face. "Don't you dare cry. Just say yes."

I did. And now Imani and I are back to planning weddings—as partners. For the first time in a long time, I'm more of a hopeless romantic than she is, which she loves. She says any man who could restore my faith in love—and weddings—is okay in her book.

Meanwhile, Clark and Emma's mom have been writing letters on behalf of an organization that advocates for putting better, more readable warnings on dangerous medications. Clark's guilt will never go away completely, but he's way more lighthearted since he started writing the letters. I had bad cramps with my period last week, and he didn't even *try* to take me to the emergency room.

Oh, yeah, and one more bit of happily ever after news... Two days after Gabe and Lucy's wedding, a piece appeared in a well-respected national magazine pointing out that Reuben has a not-so-subtle habit of stealing material from real life. The interviewer had done a little digging, and somehow discovered that Reuben had really, truly cheated on me, and used the publication of his book to let me know.

Imani sent me the article so I'd be one of the first to read it. For the first time in my life, I was extremely grateful that my humiliation was a poorly-kept secret

Two days after *that*, I heard through the grapevine that Reuben's publisher didn't offer him a new contract. Last I heard, Reuben is looking into ghostwriting memoirs for reality TV stars.

After a while Clark drifts my way, and a moment later, we're joined by Lucy and Gabe, glowing with new-marriage happiness, leaning into each other and periodically exchanging fond glances.

"Hey," Clark says to Gabe. "I owe you several apologies."

"Yeah?" Gabe asks.

"I almost bailed out on being your best man."

Gabe shrugs. "Yeah, but you didn't. Besides, even if you had, I wouldn't have held it against you. You obviously had to go get Jessa. Especially since Buck had already put his stamp of approval on her."

"No," Lucy says. "Don't do this, Gabe."

"What?" he demands, turning to her.

She spreads her hands in front of us. "He has this cockamamie idea that if Buck barfs up something belonging to a Wilder brother's girlfriend, that means it's meant to be."

Clark squints at his brother. "Please tell me you don't believe that."

"Can't do that, bro," Gabe says. "You just wait. You'll see."

"When will I see?" Clark demands.

Gabe shrugs. "I don't know. I can't see the future. Only Buck can."

"Buck can see the future," Clark repeats blandly. "So what does he have to say about that?" He inclines his head and we all turn to see Hanna and Easton arguing, hands flying in gestures of irritation and impatience.

"No," Lucy says sadly. "Those two are hopeless. Even Buck can't help them."

We all nod in acknowledgment of this fact. And then I realize that Clark isn't nodding, and he isn't looking at Hanna and Easton.

His eyes are on Kane, and there is a thoughtful look in them.

Obviously Clark owes me a story.

ACKNOWLEDGMENTS

Thank you, readers! You're my favorite part of this job, and falling in love with the Wilders alongside you has been such a delight. I'm so glad you adore Gabe, Brody, Clark, and their family and friends as much as I do.

My favorite part of doing research into Jessa's history and background was time spent with friends Soomie and Sydney Sorenson, who in addition to being the best sources of Korean drama recommendations I know of, were also indispensable guides to their particular Korean-American experience. Sydney and Soomie generously shared with me about being Korean-American in two different generations and about family, food, culture, names, weddings, and anything else I could think to ask.

Thank you to Dani Moran, who as a (thorough, thoughtful, and kind) sensitivity editor for Tessera Editorial, also contributed her perspective on her Korean-American experience.

In addition to watching way more Korean dramas than I would like to admit to, I read quite a few books I'd recommend, including *If I Had Your Face* (a novel) by Frances Cha,

The Birth of Korean Cool by Euny Hong, and *A Geek in Korea: Discovering Asia's New Kingdom of Cool* by Daniel Tudor.

Any errors of fact or insensitivity relating to representation are mine and mine alone. If you note any, please let me know so I can apologize and learn to be better.

Thank you so much to my early readers this time around, Christina Hovland, Christine D'Abo, Rachel Grant, and Susannah Nix. Thank you for taking time away from your own stories to help make this book the best it could be.

Huge thanks also to the author friends who support me on a regular basis—Dylann Crush, Megan Ryder, Dawn Luedecke, Christy, Brenda St. John Brown, Christine, Gwen Hernandez, Rachel, Kate Davies, Kris Kennedy, Karen Booth, Susannah Nix, and many, many more, including but not limited to the authors of the Corner of Smart and Sexy, Small Town World Domination, Wide for the Win, RAM Rom Com, Tinsel and Tatas, and my two ongoing newsletter swaps.

Thank you to my agent, Emily Sylvan Kim, and my sub rights agent, Tina Shen, who make magic happen all the time!

Thank you, Sarah Sarai! You have made edits one of my favorite parts of my job. I always laugh, I always learn, and thank you so much for picking up not one, not two, not three, but FOUR dropped threads in *Wilder With You*. I appreciate knowing what happened to Reuben, and I know my readers do, too. Also, I will never look at an ellipsis the same way.

Thank you, XPresso Book Tours, especially Giselle, for the release blitz!

I cannot imagine doing any of my jobs without the love and support of my amazing friends, Aimee, Chelsea, Cheryl, Darya, Ellen, Gail, Jess, Julia, Kathy, Lauren, Molly, Soomie, and Tracey.

Bell Girl, I miss you every day you're gone at college, and Bell Boy, I savor every day I have left with you. For all the times you patiently repeated a question you inadvertently asked me when I was off somewhere in Fictionland, thank you for being willing to try again. I love you most of all the people I ever made.

Mr. Bell: Romance heroes want to be you when they grow up. I love you madly.

ALSO BY SERENA BELL

Wilder Adventures

Make Me Wilder

Walk on the Wilder Side

Wilder With You

A Little Wilder

Under One Roof

Do Over

Head Over Heels

Sleepover

Returning Home

Hold On Tight

Can't Hold Back

To Have and to Hold

Holding Out

Tierney Bay

So Close

So True

So Good (2022)

So Right (2023)

New York Glitz

Still So Hot!

Hot & Bothered

Standalone

Turn Up the Heat

ABOUT THE AUTHOR

USA Today bestselling author Serena Bell writes contemporary romance with heat, heart, and humor. A former journalist, Serena has always believed that everyone has an amazing story to tell if you listen carefully, and you can often find her scribbling in her tiny garret office, mainlining chocolate and bringing to life the tales in her head.

Serena's books have earned many honors, including a RITA finalist spot, an RT Reviewers' Choice Award, Apple Books Best Book of the Month, and Amazon Best Book of the Year for Romance.

When not writing, Serena loves to spend time with her college-sweetheart husband and two hilarious kiddos—all of whom are incredibly tolerant not just of Serena's imaginary friends but also of how often she changes her hobbies and how passionately she embraces the new ones. These days, it's stand-up paddle boarding, board-gaming, meditation, and long walks with good friends.

Manufactured by Amazon.com.au
Sydney, New South Wales, Australia